Factory
of
Death

Kathleen Anne Fleming

Kathleen Anne Fleming

Published by **Washington House**
A division of Trident Media Company
801 N Pitt Street, Suite 123
Alexandria, VA 22314 USA

To my husband,
John Terzis, and my children,
Clare and Nicholas.

CHAPTER ONE

Robby Saxony jiggled the keys in the double front door lock of the converted loft offices of Saxony Clothiers. The former factory was located in the heart of Northwoods, an affluent town on the North Shore of Chicago. He dropped them then, and cursed the early cold fall weather which had reached only forty degrees on this late October night. His hands were stiff from the cold. The keys smacked loudly on the concrete.

Finally he barreled through the thick door and raced across an endless hardwood floor. Located on the fourth floor of the factory, his office encompassed half the square footage, while the other half was used for photography shoots and troubleshooting with the latest hemlines.

Once in his office, he pushed the speaker phone button and called his wife at their home in Glen Ayre, a neighboring town to Northwoods.

"Hello?" Her voice was husky.

"Brandy? Look. I forgot some paperwork for a meeting on Monday so I had to come back."

"Fine."

"Don't give me that tone of voice, Brandy. I'm telling you the truth."

"That's a switch."

"So I'll be about an hour."

"Why so long?"

"I have to go through some paperwork here and then I have to stop at the pharmacy on the way home."

"Fine, Robby. I'll have Sestina keep dinner warm. It's her late night. She'll be with Charlie. I'm going out with the girls." She smiled, hoping to irk him.

Memo in hand, he was only half interested. "Again?" he said. "Goodbye, Robby."

He held the phone for an extended moment, the delay due to disinterest. He'd not noticed right away that she was no longer on the line.

Flipping through a stack full of memos from the day, he made notes in pencil. He insisted that his assistant, Elizabeth, always maintain ten sharp pencils on his desk each morning.

Without thinking, he hit his speed dial and waited a perfunctory two rings.

"Hi, lover," a soprano voice said through his speaker phone.

"Want a late dinner tonight?"

"How about here at my place. We'll skip dinner."

"I look forward to it," he said, looking up from his paperwork to smirk.

That's when he heard something.

"I have to go," he said.

Standing, he shoved his paperwork into his briefcase and crept over to his office door which he'd left ajar. Then he heard it—a tormented but faint scream from somewhere across the floor.

Racing out, he first checked the hallway to the right which led to the elevators, then turned back. The voice had echoed throughout the place, the building being a former loft, which confused his bearings. The restrooms were the only spots left. He crept to the left of the floor, searching the copy room. Turning back down the hallway at the end of the high ceilinged foyer, he stopped short.

Extending out from the ladies room door he spied a familiar set of legs, one leg straightened all the way out the door, the other one bent. She still wore the blue suit he always liked on her. Next to the body was a telltale two-inch pump shoe he recognized. Looking around quickly, he stepped toward the body, leaned over, and pushed the bathroom door open gently. He felt for a pulse and soon had no doubt that Elizabeth was dead.

Backing away, he stumbled for the exit doors and, once opened, checked the hallways, then took the stairs down four flights, his hands scraping the raw brick walls as he panted to the point of hyperventilating.

His black Jaguar XJ6 was there. He'd not locked it. No one was supposed to have been at the office that night. Barreling down Willow Road toward Glen Ayre, his mind worked frantically. Elizabeth. He had known her well. Elizabeth Marx had been the head of the administrators for Saxony skirts, now called Saxony Clothiers. Why would anyone murder Elizabeth, for God's sake?

Within minutes he whipped down a street with a dangling white sign that read "Park Drive, Private, No entry." Following the gravel drive, he drove on, without focus, ruminating. He'd turned down the hard rock station he'd switched on and soon came to an iron gate. The front gate was inscribed with the oversized initials "RS." Then he drove up yet another cobblestone drive to an audaciously large house, the result of newer construction; the house had two spires, in English Tudor style, one to the left and one on the right of a massive red door.

It was now 10:30 P.M. exactly. The only light visible in the house emanated from the kitchen. He discerned the slight and slender silhouette of Sestina, their nanny and maid. His four- year-old son Charlie often called her "mommy." Robby noticed it never fazed Brandy that her only child gravitated to Sestina rather than to herself.

He entered the foyer. "Sestina? Is that you? Is Brandy home?" He tried to sound routine.

Sestina rushed into the hallway wiping her hands with a dish towel. "Mr. Saxony. You frightened me. I didn't hear you drive up."

Sestina was lithe and blonde, and as usual wore her black stretch pants and tight little avocado green turtleneck. Robby had tried on numerous occasions to get intimate with Sestina, but being a woman of the old country, she had made it clear that since she'd left Poland three years before, she had been determined to make it on her own in the new country of America.

"I've just finished up the laundry and dishes. Charlie is asleep. Mrs. Saxony is out for the evening. I'm to bed now for a book and a bath. Is there anything else?"

"No, Sestina," he said, massaging his forehead with his hands. "I'm pretty worn out, too."

"You look very tired, Mr. Saxony. Is everything fine with you? You look very pale."

Two hours later, Jan Gates lay awake. Although she often stayed up reading past midnight, tonight she was simply restless. She got up

9

and started begrudgingly on the dishes.

She looked out the sink window to the enormous main house built in the 1920s. The owner of the house, who had rented Jan the coach house, was horrified by the new monstrosity they had built across the street on Park Drive. She'd attended all the zoning meetings to fight it. Still, the thing was built.

From the coach house window Jan turned out all the lights around her and then opened the shade over her sink. She had spotted him in his three-car garage across the street. It was around 12:15 A.M. Mr. Robby Saxony roamed about his gratuitous garage rubbing his head with his fingertips. Jan noticed he was chain-smoking and pacing. She had heard from his wife Brandy, the week before, that he had finally quit just that week. Brandy Saxony often became very chatty after a night out with the girls, as if all the pretty umbrella drinks from the local pick-up tavern still swam in her veins.

Now Robby sat on the back fender of his Lexus SUV truck, and stamped out another cigarette. Although a nice vehicle, he usually drove his black Jaguar XJ6. After another twenty minutes, Jan grew tired of watching her neighbor in his high class angst. She went to bed.

Hours later, Jan slammed her hand on the alarm clock. Rolling into the kitchen, she yawned as she rinsed out a water glass then she caught a quick breath. Across the street which led to the Saxony house, she spotted Robby. Except this time he was lying on the cement floor of the garage. Jan panicked. What had happened to him?

She dialed 911.

"Yes. My neighbor at 99 Park Lane here in Glen Ayre. He's collapsed. I mean, I don't know what's wrong with him. Could you send an ambulance?"

"Have you talked to anyone at his home?" the operator asked.

"No. I'll do that now."

"What makes you think he's injured? Don't worry, I've already sent an ambulance. I'm just wondering."

"Well, this is embarrassing," she paused. "I was up late last night. I noticed him in his three-car garage pacing around and smoking. You see, he just quit smoking. So I know he must have been upset to already be smoking again. His wife Brandy told me he had just quit. But I'll just go over there. Thanks for your help."

As she finished speaking, an ambulance was heard at the end of the street. Jan raced across the street and was concerned to see that Robby's body was no longer in the garage.

"How am I going to explain this?" she said aloud, her mouth agape as she stepped across the cold hard lawn.

The ambulance and two squad cars pulled up, screeching and shrill, telling the neighborhood that some sort of unlikely and odd experience had occurred. This was a town that rarely suffered hang-nails, much less murders.

"I'm the one who phoned," Jan said as the first squad car pulled up. "I don't know what to say."

Behind her, Brandy Saxony stepped out of the massive front door between the two spires, wearing a Victoria's Secret bathrobe made for an even a smaller woman. It was white on the inside and covered with wild flowers on the outside.

"What the hell is going on here?" she demanded.

"Brandy," Jan said, racing up, her arms extended. "You won't believe what I thought I saw."

"What?"

"Miss," the first police officer on the scene said, struggling to avoid her bare legs and look her in the eyes. "What's going on here? You said you saw someone in distress? Or a body? Is that right?"

"Brandy," Jan whispered furiously, "I thought I saw Robby."

Brandy ran her fingers through her multibleached blonde-red hair. "Well, I'm sure you see him everyday coming and going. What's the difference?"

"Are you Mrs. Saxony?" the police officer asked.

"Yes, I am. Look, Robby didn't come home last night."

Jan's eyes widened. A sick feeling washed over her. Was someone lying or did she imagine Robby Saxony on the floor of his garage?

"I know I saw him there," Jan said, pointing.

Brandy yawned and messed her hair with her hands. "Jan, you seem to see a lot of things you shouldn't."

The officer frowned. "What time did you see Mr. Saxony?" he asked.

Again the embarrassment. "Around midnight, the first time."

Brandy shook her head, then cracked open a Diet Pepsi and took a long sip. One detective eyed her intently from top to bottom.

"I'll admit," she said, "I got home after 2 A.M."

"You were out for the evening, miss?" the officer asked.

"Mrs. Saxony. Yes, I was out."

"Do you and your husband often take separate evenings out?"

Brandy bristled. "What is this all about? I have a right to go out where I want, don't I? You don't even have a body, for God's sake."

"If the lady thought she saw one, we have to check it out. You understand. Where would your husband be now?" the officer asked, checking his watch. "It's 5 A.M. Does he usually go in this early? Is there a chance you missed him?"

"Take a look at the size of this house," she said sharply. "I suppose I could miss him here."

"Why don't you give him a call at the office?" the first officer said. "Do you mind if we have a look around anyway? We have to when there's been a report like this."

The ambulances cleared out after a thorough search of the garage and a quick look through the house. Jan approached the officers.

"What is your name?" she asked. "In case I need to call again."

"I'm Detective Pargulski," he said. He had dark curly hair and hazel eyes. "Yeah. Go ahead and call me again. You'll make my day."

"I'm sorry," Jan said, walking swiftly about, clearly mortified at her mistake. "But I know what I saw. Why did they have you come over, detective? I mean, instead of just the police?"

"Possible homicide in Glen Ayre? You bet they call me in."

Brandy stepped outside again and waved to Detective Pargulski.

"Look, I reached him at the office. He's fine. Thank you for all your trouble."

The detective nodded, then signaled to the other squad car to clear out. Brandy strolled back inside but her face grew grim once the front door slammed behind her.

Stalking to the phone in the kitchen she picked it up again. "They're gone, you ass. So you want to explain what's going on? Jan Gates, our crazy little coach house artist across the street, says she saw you. Was this a trick of hers out of boredom? The woman is a crazy person."

"No, Brandy. Just listen for once. I actually was in the garage in the middle of the night. I woke up at around four this morning. I showered and came in to work. You, of course, were passed out on the bed."

Brandy spilled a bottle of Tylenol as she listened. Her head was pounding. Her mouth tasted of rotten cotton. "Keep your voice down. Don't yell."

"I'm not. As usual you're hung over."

"What do you care? Who else is at your office at this hour anyway?"

"No one. That's why I came in early."

Yet as he spoke, a piercing scream echoed throughout the hallway.

"What the hell was that?" Brandy asked.

"I have to go," he said, slamming the phone down.

He had to remind himself to act as if he'd not seen the murdered woman. He'd not be prepared for what the body looked like now. A young woman crouched over the body.

"What is it, Amanda?" he said to his sister, the senior vice president of marketing with an executive office down the hall from his.

"Call 911!" she said.

At the sight, however, he stood there, dumbfounded. The woman, Elizabeth Marx, had been his assistant for the past year and a half. She was different from the way he'd found her dead hours before. And next to the body was a brown wooden figurine. It depicted a woman with fire flames shooting out behind her. She now wore a long skirt, with puffy sleeves, and she had gloves on her stiff hands. Robby was stunned. Who had tampered with the body?

"Is she still alive?" he said.

"We should at least call 911!"

Her voice was angry. Racing to a secretary's desk he picked up a phone and dialed. Fifteen minutes passed and paramedics arrived. Some time later, detectives and the coroner showed up.

Amanda waltzed into her brother's office and slammed the door shut behind her.

"What the hell has happened to your assistant?"

"You're asking me?" he said, standing behind his massive chair, his hand leaving a damp imprint on the leather.

"She was your assistant."

"What was she wearing?" he asked.

"Wearing? She's dead for God's sake, Robby!"

13

He shook his head, running his hand through his thick black hair. He paced to the window and looked out over the green and manicured corporate acres. "Keep your voice down," he said sternly. "I just don't get why she was wearing those clothes."

"They said she's been dead at least five hours. That would mean she met someone here in the middle of the night. I know that's your routine with the assistants on watch, right?"

"You're not helpful. And if this is how you keep talking around everyone, I'll end up in jail. I had nothing to do with this. She was at the place across the street for her birthday. Some people from work took her out."

"What do you know about Elizabeth?" she asked pointedly.

"She worked in the loop downtown for a while. She went around with a wild bunch from what she told me."

"Someone wild enough to want to kill her?" Amanda pursued.

"How would I know?"

"I would think you'd want to know. You're going to be the prime suspect, I can tell you that much."

Robby sat slouched at his desk. His phone rang and, on reflex, he picked it up quickly. "What is it?"

It was Sandy, an assistant from a nearby desk. "Excuse me Robby. It's your uncle. Mr. Joseph Saxony is on the phone."

"I'll call him back," he said gruffly.

"Are you sure you won't speak to him? He wants to know about," she hesitated, "the death."

"I'll call him back," he finished, slamming the phone down.

Amanda stood up, clicking her heels together. Her suit was a seafoam green and her tights matched the hue. She had her white blonde hair pulled back into a tight bun at the back of her head.

"Get your story straight, Robby. Everyone is going to be looking at you, asking you questions. And I guess you and I had better get the story straight as a team. They're going to be looking to me too, God knows."

"You're talking like a crazy person. I had nothing to do with Elizabeth's death."

"Who else would have been here in the middle of the night? Brandy said you were here late."

There was a loud knock on the door. Robby had adjusted the

vertical blinds for privacy along the large plate glass window.
"Come in," he said irritably.
Amanda stepped back, trying to appear unruffled. She studied a
memo in her hand, straining to be professional. It was the assistant
from the senior vice president's office down the hall.
"Mr. Titus would like to see you, Robby," Sandy said. "He needs
to know about this whole," her voice wavered, "mishap. I don't know
what to call it. It's just so tragic. Who would want to kill Elizabeth?"
"Thank you, Sandy," he said. "Tell him I'll be right there."
He said it as smoothly as if he'd agreed to meet another executive
for an ad hoc committee meeting. Could the stain of murder just go
away if he ignored it?
"What I don't get," he whispered tersely to Amanda, "is what was
she wearing. Elizabeth, I mean. That wasn't what—she couldn't have
been wearing those clothes before she was killed?"
Amanda scrutinized him. "Why not? It's time to examine her
friends, her co-workers, and anyone you can think of."
"Why are you so insistent on this point?" he asked, clearly
annoyed.
"Because Elizabeth called me at 11:30 last night."

CHAPTER TWO

Jan Gates stood shivering on the front doorstep of Glenda Morgan's bungalow. She buzzed the doorbell again, looking left and right. Autumn had hit early. And on this Chicago morning, the crisp bite of winter already filled her nostrils. Then she heard the locks working on the old prairie-style front door of Glenda's house and she shook straggly bangs out of her eyes.

"Jan?" Glenda said, blinking and fighting a yawn.

"I am so sorry to just show up," Jan said, then broke into tears.

"My God, come in. What's going on?" She put an arm around her shoulder and led her friend inside. Grabbing a throw from the sofa, she wrapped it around her. "Whatever it is, a good cup of coffee and a talk will straighten things out."

Jan threw herself back into a straight-back chair and buried her face in her hands. Her hair was swept up in a plastic clip on the top of her head. She wore a terry-cloth bathrobe under her coat.

"I knew I shouldn't have watched them so much. It's just that when Sandy called me this morning I knew something was really going on."

"With whom?" Glenda asked, spooning dried coffee into the filter of her Krups coffee maker.

"My neighbor. You know. I know I've told you about them. Brandy and Robby Saxony? They live in this huge monstrosity, a McMansion they call them, where they build as much square footage as they can squeeze onto an acre of land. Well, last night I saw Robby in his garage at around midnight. I've seen the two of them fight many times, but this time—this was different. I know I saw him alive in his garage at midnight. But then at 4:30 A.M., I saw his body just lying there on the floor. So I called the police."

"Well, that was wise. Then what happened? Was he dead?"

Glenda poured coffee for Jan and then added creamer, the way she knew her friend liked it.

"It was awful. The ambulances came and the police swarmed the place. You know how it is in Glen Ayre. Nothing ever happens. So the cops just show up by the truckload and go crazy. Well, then Brandy came outside and she says he probably just went to work. So she went inside and called him and he was at his office."

Glenda whistled and shook her head. "Embarrassing, was it?"

Jan nodded, her tears slowing down. "I thought that was it. But then I got a phone call from Sandy. You know, my friend Sandy Larson? She works at Robby's company—Saxony Clothiers. They made the old factory in Northwoods into the corporate office.

"Well, she called me to tell me there was a murder at the Saxony office. Very quiet. She said Saxony was trying to keep it all hush-hush—you know, no press. But she had to tell someone. The police were there asking all kinds of questions, trying to find out who was at the office around the time of the murder."

"What did they narrow it down to? And do you know if the detective from the Glen Ayre force was there?"

"I don't know who the cop was. But the murder they said had to have happened in the middle of the night. The victim was strangled. I don't know. It's all so confusing."

"What else is upsetting you?" Glenda said, touching her hand gently.

"Well, Robby was acting so strangely when I saw him. That was at midnight. And the murdered woman was his assistant."

"So you think he may have been involved?"

"That's just it," Jan said, looking up, her eyes red. "I don't know the concrete details. But I do know what time it was and that Robby looked upset. He may have just come from the office or he could have been getting ready to leave. I don't know. How do I explain to anyone why I was watching the house at midnight? And then again at four o'clock this morning? Does anyone understand insomnia? They're going to think I'm a voyeur or stalker or something."

Glenda laughed lightly. "Who cares? You told the police. You did the right thing."

"But what if I'm completely wrong and I get an innocent man suspected?"

"What else did your friend Sandy say?"

Glenda brought over a box of blue kleenex to the table. Jan grabbed two tissues.

"Is Sandy a reliable person?"

"What do you mean?"

"I mean, is she the type of person who would be accurate with information?"

"Yes. But what she told me is so unbelievable. The woman was an assistant to Robby. But what they found her wearing..." Jan said, stuttering as she tried to talk. "She was wearing a long skirt—but not just a long skirt like you'd see around now. It was a Victorian Saxony skirt and she had on a matching blouse from 1900 or so."

"Maybe she was in some sort of show for the company?"

Jan looked up, her face red. She shook her head. "No. The name in the blouse was Eliza Mortimer."

"And who was she?"

"I don't know. Someone from the past of the Saxony Skirt company. I think whoever killed her was playing a sick prank."

Glenda nodded. Patting her friend on the back, she walked to her small library which she'd made in the front of the house. Scanning the shelves, she found two books on the Glen Ayre and Rosedale histories that the historical society had put out several years before.

"What I don't get," Jan went on, "was why someone would want to kill Robby's assistant. Sandy was really shook up. So, I gather, were all the other assistants over there."

"I assume they're all women?" Glenda asked, grinning.

"Well, yes, they are. The company, from what I've heard, has always been kind of for the good old boys. You know, the old money management style. Women move up there, but it's a slow process. And they only go so far."

Jan's expression softened as she started to calm down. She sipped her coffee with a small smile, the steam rising from the cup as she set it down.

"Perfect on the cream, Glenda. Thanks."

"I remembered only because you like your coffee like I do." She smiled and sat down, plopping several large books down on the dining room table. "These are books on the history of the area around here. I'm sure there's got to be something in here about the Saxony company." She scanned the pages with her forefinger. "Here, for instance, is a one-page story about them."

Jan nodded, looking uncertain. "I'm going to get more coffee. Want a refresher?"

"Sure," Glenda said, handing over a cup.

Glenda started to read to herself from the history books, and then grew quiet. She continued to read even after Jan had returned to the room.

"What is it? Read it to me." Jan said.

"It's just about one Saxony man after another taking over the helm of the company. Then there's a little blurb about Robby and his sister's involvement. Amanda Saxony is more active in the company too. She's the only woman on the board of directors and that's only because of her lineage."

She set the book aside and took a sip of coffee. Jan stared at her an extra second. Glenda sensed Jan could not handle the rest of it yet. She let her hand rest on the book.

"I don't know if you want to hear it all."

"Come on, Glenda."

Glenda flipped the book open to the page again. "It says there was a young woman named Eliza Mortimer. They refer to her as 'Eliza the Slasher.'"

"What?" her voice was strained.

"She was hanged for the murder of William Saxony. There's an implied relationship between the two. But she is definitely made out to be a villain. William was a married man and left behind a young wife named Fanny, and five children. Only one of those five was a son, who was of course the grandfather of our good Robby Saxony."

"What a gruesome history," Jan agreed. "Sandy warned me about Amanda Saxony. She's a corporate monster. I guess she works around the clock. It was no secret that Amanda ran into Robby's office this morning and there was some yelling going on. The police questioned Robby, Amanda, and another assistant who got in very early, to discuss Elizabeth's death. Still, they couldn't place anyone there precisely when she was murdered. God, it's just so awful."

"What puzzles me," Glenda said, "is that you saw Robby Saxony in his garage for as long as you did. Because then his wife claimed he never came home?"

"That's right. But what would she know. I hate to say it, but

Brandy Saxony is known for her binge nights out. Their marriage is not a good one—I mean if I can even tell that and I'm a neighbor, imagine what goes on behind closed doors."

Glenda nodded, thoughtful a moment. "And they have a son? Charlie?"

"Yes. He's five."

"There's a lot more I'll need to know if I'm going to help you. Why don't we meet for dinner tonight, Jan. Maybe we can dig a little deeper."

Jan nodded. "I feel so involved. I've known Robby Saxony since junior high school. And Sandy is really upset."

"I have to get back to my store. Remember my place? It's called 'In Retrospect.'"

"Yes, I do. I hear it's doing well."

"Business is good," Glenda said, nodding. "You sure you're up to driving home?"

"Sure."

"Why don't we meet at Antonio's tonight? Around seven?"

Jan nodded. She pulled her coat on over her blue terry- cloth bathrobe.

An hour later, Glenda was reviewing inventory in the back of her antique shop. Putsying around, she didn't notice the small bell jingling over the front door of the shop. But then she noted the voices of two young women.

"I'm in back if you need me," Glenda said so they could hear.

"We're just looking," came a woman's voice. Glenda could hear their conversation.

"So anyway, Gwen, it's all very creepy around the office. No one can work, of course. Except Robby and the executives. They never stop. The police, of course, have the area roped off."

"So it was Amanda Saxony who was murdered?"

"No, oh no. It was Robby Saxony's assistant. There were rumors, you know. They were having an affair or something, the murdered woman, Elizabeth Marx, and Robby."

"Look at this old camera," the first woman said.

"It's really old, I'd say," said the other woman.

Glenda straightened up, pressing her hand to the small of her back. She knew it would be beneficial to reach for items on the floor the proper way, by bending her knees and not leaning over, but she never did. And her back always paid for it. Then a snippet of conversation caught her attention.

"Let's ask the owner of the place. Excuse us? We have a question for you."

Glenda stepped out from behind a shelf at the back of the shop, wiping dust off her blackwatch plaid skirt.

"Hi. I'm the proprietor. What do you need?"

"Look at this camera," the shorter woman said. "Do you know how old it is?"

Glenda walked over, smiling. "You know what? My assistant Mindy went to an estate sale last week." She stroked the top of the wooden object, tracing the black label on its top with her fingertip. It rested on top of a black tripod and stood about three feet high.

"So Mindy must have picked this up. I haven't priced these items yet. But are you interested in it?" she asked.

The taller woman, a brunette, shook her head. "No, we're just curious about it."

"Do you two work around town?" Glenda asked, already knowing the answer.

"Why, yes," the brunette said. "We work at Saxony Clothiers. The corporate office location in Northwoods."

Glenda nodded, her eyes on the two. "I heard there was a murder there."

Both women looked visibly shaken. "I'm Glenda Morgan, by the way. I've known the Saxony name since I was a kid."

"I'm Sandy Larson," the brunette said. "This is my friend, Gwen."

"Pleased to meet you," Glenda said. "I think we have a mutual friend. Jan Gates?"

Sandy's face mellowed. "You're Glenda! It's good to meet you."

"She's the one who told me about the trouble at Saxony Clothiers."

Sandy nodded somberly. "I was familiar with Elizabeth—the woman who was murdered. We weren't friends but I did know a lot about her and her life. She was really determined to move up at the company. I guess some thought she went about it the wrong way."

Glenda nodded. She took a dust cloth from behind the front desk and wiped the camera down gently. "May I ask what you mean by the 'wrong way'?"

Sandy exchanged a look with Gwen. "She became really close with her boss. Too close, in many a person's opinion. He's a married man after all."

Glenda nodded. "How long did she work for him, do you know?"

"At least three years, because she was already there when I started, which was a little over two years ago. At first it was known by everyone that she worked long hours. That's why it didn't seem strange that Elizabeth would have been at the office during off hours."

"But I heard Robby wasn't even in until after the murder took place. At around 7 A.M.?"

"We really should be getting back to work," Gwen said, rather strangely.

She sounded afraid, somehow.

"You're right," Sandy said, grabbing her purse from a nearby table.

Glenda continued to wax the table with the cloth in circular motions, her thoughts not on the camera but rather sizing up the two women.

"Thanks for your help," Sandy said. "I'm sure we'll be back. It's a wonderful shop."

Glenda walked them to the door and saw them out. Turning back to the shop, something about the camera caught her eye. Leaning over, she examined it—looking underneath the camera. There was something next to the tripod legs. A name was inscribed in black letters, "William Saxony."

How can this be? she wondered. As she thought this, the front door jingled again. Mindy strolled in, coming back from lunch.

"Mindy, do you know where this camera came from?"

"Fom the Peacock estate," Mindy said, as she set a bag of fries behind an ancient cash register. "Some woman brought in a few items about a week ago," she said.

"Do you recall her name, by any chance?"

Mindy grabbed a black address book she kept at the side of the register. "Let me see," she said, flipping through the pages. "A Mrs. Brandy Saxony."

Glenda's eyes widened. "Really?"

"Why? Do you know her?"

23

Glenda nodded with a half smile. "My friend Jan is messed up in their family troubles lately. There was a strange-sounding murder at Saxony Clothiers last night. It's got everyone in Rosedale and Glen Ayre blown away. And, you know, nothing out of the ordinary happens here. When it does, the whole North Shore is talking."

Mindy tossed the french fry bag in the garbage container under the desk. She pulled her short brown hair back in a ponytail. "I did hear a quick blurb on the radio. The name hit me because this Brandy Saxony woman had just come in last week. Do you think there's a connection?"

Glenda was thoughtful. "Could be. I've come to regard coincidences carefully. I take them as messages, if you know what I mean."

"I know. It's your theory on life that everything happens for a reason."

Glenda walked casually to a set of white wicker furniture and sat down. She whipped through receipts from a drawer by the front desk. "I just heard something about Brandy Saxony and the Saxony family. It's got a couple of people pretty upset—something about old William having taken some lewd shots for the time."

Glenda walked back to the camera and picked it up, turning it upside down to examine it. "You know, in the old days they sent the cameras directly to the Kodak laboratories to get the film developed. This one reads, Pinewood, Illinois. That's way up in the northwestern suburbs."

"Maybe we should call there and see if there's still a store up there. Maybe they can even tell you something about the camera or its owner," Mindy said.

"Let's go one better than that. I'm going to call to see if they still exist and visit there in person."

"Who were those young women I saw leaving the store?" Mindy asked.

"They're my connections over at Saxony Clothiers. I feel bad for my friend Jan. I mean, she's always been an active person. But unfortunately, she gets too involved in people's lives."

"You mean a busybody?" Mindy said, smiling.

"You could call it that. But she has good intentions. I have a special understanding for her too. You see, Jan suffers from depression. She's struggled with it for years. But she sees a therapist regularly."

"You're so up on all this psychology stuff."

"Well, I know you're going to think this is strange. But I've always heard dubious stories about Saxony Clothiers. It's the way they treat their employees. I say this because there were two women just in here that were acting somewhat strangely— especially Jan's friend Sandy."

"Why don't you talk to Jan about it?"

"We're meeting for dinner tonight. How about a field trip with me this weekend?" Glenda asked.

"You want to hit the northwest suburbs, don't you?"

"I think it would help to do a little historical research. And I'd like to allay some of Jan's fears. She is really upset about the whole ordeal."

As she spoke, Glenda rummaged through the box of items left by Brandy Saxony. "Wonder why she wanted to unload all this stuff. What's your take on it, Mindy?"

"Not sure. But what a character that Brandy woman is. She had on a pink Gucci running suit and a ponytail on top of her head. She was acting really nervous too."

"What's going on with the Saxony family, I wonder."

Just as Glenda said this, she discovered a brown file folder with a string tied around it in the bottom of the box. After she opened it, she took a quick breath. An array of photographs fell to the floor. Glenda breezed through numerous shots of an attractive woman in glasses. She wore a long white frilly dress. But then the last photo caught her eye. It was definitely someone else. Definitely someone with evil in her eyes.

CHAPTER THREE

Jan wrung her hands over and over, itching the left one repeatedly, leaving a red blotch next to her thumb. Glenda noticed they looked dry.

"Jan, you're really nervous."

"I can't believe I'm part of this whole Saxony mess. Brandy was out in her garage half of this afternoon after I saw you. I don't know what she was doing."

Glenda smiled.

"I know. You think I'm a shameless peeping Tom, don't you?"

"Jan, I've known you a long time. I know that you wouldn't be alarmed unless there was something strange going on. Like, remember in college, when all the kids on your floor were planning some horrible prank? And you knew someone could have gotten hurt? Something about explosives and breaking into the biology lab."

"I was pretty blown away. And it was my boyfriend planning the whole scheme."

"But you kept your cool. So I know this Saxony murder must be really extraordinary for you to get upset about it."

Jan nodded, sipping her iced tea. "It's just I've known them as a couple since before their son Charlie was born. In fact, I've even sat for Charlie before they got their nanny Sestina. Of course, I've known Robby since junior high school when I moved to Glen Ayre."

Glenda smiled when the waitress brought over her caesar salad and another round of iced teas. "And it's interesting too that Mindy received a large donation from Brandy not too long ago. But oddly, she barely gave a word of warning. Just showed up and left a boxload of stuff at the store."

"Interesting."

Then Jan's eyes spotted some new patrons who'd just walked in the door.

"My God."

"What is it?" Glenda said.

"I haven't seen her in a while but I think that's Amanda Saxony." Glenda started to turn.

"Don't look. She's even scarier than Robby."

Glenda was able to catch a glimpse of the two as they passed her table. From the back she could have thought it was two men, but then Amanda turned and was seated facing Glenda.

Amanda had her hair pulled back in her signature tight bun. Not a single white-blonde strand was loose. She had high-arched eyebrows and a serious demeanor. And Amanda's companion appeared to be somewhat younger, perhaps in his early twenties.

"Do you know the young man?" Glenda asked.

"I didn't get a look. Try not to look at her."

Glenda frowned. "Are you afraid of her?"

"To be honest, I've only met her once. It was at a lavish Christmas party the Saxonys had several years ago. They'd invited the entire neighborhood, anxious to impress everyone. They'd just had this monstrous house built in the middle of all these classic old homes and then they threw this outlandish party. There were chauffeured limousines, a man providing costumes at the door like it was Mardi Gras, waiters wielding petit fours, locked storage for all the furs, and of course, caviar—and that was all before dinner."

Jan leaned forward more and more with each little bit she described to her friend.

"So what did you learn about Amanda that night?"

"First of all," Jan said, lowering her voice, "Amanda spoke only to the businessmen—you know, there were guys from the Chicago Mercantile Exchange and the Board of Trade. Kind of the good-old-boy network. Most of the wives were wearing their lace and gold lame, and there was Amanda, in her usual severe black pants suit and her blonde hair pulled back way too tightly. I don't think there were any women in business or the arts there except myself and Amanda."

"Well, that's just how she looks. Tell me what she's like."

Jan was thoughtful, playing with her bangs.

"She's very outspoken about everything."

"Has it always been a Saxony-owned business?"

"It was Saxony Skirts for years. But the family controlled it."

"Interesting," Glenda mused. "She has a distinct way about her. Kind of the old money thing going on. From what I've heard, the family has an older estate, a massive old brick home covered in ivy where the parents used to live. It's a castle built around 1900. It has a courtyard in the middle of it. I attended a benefit there years ago. They had a silent auction. In fact I bought a few pieces that night. I remember there were a lot of heavy drapes and the classic dresses, clothes made in the finest style for the early 1980s."

"Truth be known," Jan said quietly, "Saxony Skirts probably designed and had made those clothes. But something has always been a little strange."

Glenda watched Amanda Saxony covertly, looking up over her sips of tea now and then. "Strange? In what way?"

"There's always been a male-managed feel to the place."

"Maybe that explains Ms. Amanda's severe mannerisms," Glenda said and then was quiet. "I've heard some bizarre history about the family too. There was someone named Eliza Mortimer. She was apparently one woman who tried to get ahead back when the company was young."

"Yes, that was soon after the company was started." Jan turned around to grab a quick glance at Amanda and her companion. "That's John Mills," she said. "He's an executive at Saxony. I only know that because Sandy went out with him a couple of times. I wonder what he's doing here with her? First of all, I'm surprised that she would lower herself to be seen with a man from the company. She's an independent person who seldom is accompanied by anyone. In fact, I don't think she'd bother to have a meal with anyone unless it would improve her corporate position somehow."

"That's harsh, but true, isn't it?" Glenda agreed. "But that's how she presents herself."

Then they heard the conversation grow louder. There was a clatter of silverware and then a glass dropping to the floor.

"Tell me!" Amanda said, clearly annoyed.

Her companion murmured something. Then suddenly he pounded his hand on the table. This fired her up even more.

"As usual, John, I'm certain you know more about Robby that night than you're telling me." Then she stopped, looking left and right, realizing she'd raised her voice too high. She waved to the

29

waitress for more wine.

"Sounds like they're having a bad time," Glenda said. "Look Jan, Mindy and I are taking a trip to River Falls."

"Where's that?"

"It's in northwest Illinois. There's a cottage there. It's where Eliza Mortimer and William Saxony supposedly used to meet. She was a laborer in the factory when they started an affair. He was married. His wife's name was Fanny."

"What is there to find out if it's just an old cabin? I heard Eliza, his mistress, was very unstable. They called her 'Eliza the Slasher,' for God's sake," Jan said.

"I think there's some truth to it, maybe, some not."

Then the voices carried over to their table again. Other patrons dabbed nervously at their mouths with linen napkins.

"Don't you dare shut me out, John! How the hell do you think you got your little promotion last month? You owe me. You know that. This is not just Robby's reputation we're talking about. It's how it will look in public. He knew the girl. He knew Elizabeth Marx very well. She was his assistant. 'She types 120 words a minute,' he told me when he hired her. I knew his intentions."

Glenda leaned forward toward her friend. "How well does your friend at Saxony know Robby?"

"Sandy's desk," she whispered, "is right outside the office next to his. She saw all the comings and goings in Robby's office. There was a lot of talk about Robby and his assistant. Meetings behind closed doors, you know, with just the two of them that would last for over an hour."

"Was Elizabeth's affair with Robby common knowledge?"

"Pretty much. Look, I'll give Sandy a call right now and see what the latest is."

"Use my cell phone," Glenda said, handing a tiny Nokia over to her. "I hate to miss any action here at the next table."

Jan dialed carefully, having to clear it out and start over several times. "These little phones are so hard to dial."

Glenda simply watched the other couple. By now Amanda was standing. She threw her napkin onto the table and, with that, stalked out of the room.

"We definitely have to go to River Falls," Glenda said.

"Hello, Sandy?" Then Jan's face dropped. "What?"
Jan listened intently, following each word with a narrowing and then widening of her eyes.

"You're sure that's what he was doing? It just sounds too suspicious. Of course I know you're qualified. But what about Mr. Neil, your old boss? I guess they'll find someone else."

After she hung up, she stared at nothing for a minute. Glenda nodded when the waitress took their plates. The man who'd been sitting with Amanda Saxony was filling out the totals on his credit card bill.

"What is it, Jan?"

"It's just strange."

The waitress came by.

"May I have a cup of coffee with cream?" Jan asked.

"Me too," Glenda said.

"Well, Sandy used to work for Mr. Neil. Mr. Neil's office was located next door to Robby Saxony's. But Robby is the highest paid and still the youngest executive of all. He pretty much gets the pick of the assistants he wants. So he's asked Sandy to work for him. Mr. Neil has no choice but to go along with it. But I don't know why Sandy has agreed to it. She can't stand Robby. And she said Elizabeth was often brought to tears by the end of a work day."

"Imagine if she hadn't been sleeping with him?" Glenda mused. "But wouldn't it be a promotion for Sandy?" she asked, sipping her coffee.

"Yes, it would. But Sandy is a complex character. She's always been curious about Robby while, at the same time, been afraid of him. He's notorious in so many ways."

"And he's married," Glenda said. "How is he scary? Does he overwork his subordinates?"

"Well, with the way sexual harassment is such a public issue, he never gets accused exactly or, if he is, the human resources department helps sweep it under the rug. He also wields mental control over his subordinates and co-executives, from what I hear."

"You're really upset that Sandy has taken this position? Do you think it's too much for her? Or that she will get hurt in some way?"

"To be honest, both. She's only been there a little over two years. I don't think she understands how underhanded Robby is in everything he does."

Glenda studied Jan carefully, the clear blue eyes and petite features. There was more there. She just couldn't figure out what it was.

"How well do you know Robby and Brandy Saxony? How long have you been in Glen Ayre?"

Jan was startled. "I've lived in the coach house for six years. They built their house five years ago. I still look at Brandy and Robby as just having moved in to the neighborhood. And believe me, I've seen a number of occurrences over there."

"Such as what?"

"Well, one early evening a couple of summers ago, Brandy had a party for her friends. You could tell this did not include the Saxony side of the family. Let's just say things got pretty heated. Aside from it being above 90 degrees that day, Robby was apparently just unbearable. One by one, Brandy's angry friends disappeared in their little pick-up trucks. One young brutish man in particular Brandy followed out to his white Cutlass. They stood there, talking quite intimately for at least half an hour. Well, Robby finally came outside and called her a slut or something. She started throwing comments, and her shoes if I remember, at him. So I guess it was at that point that I realized they weren't the most compatible couple."

"Do you remember what happened next?" Glenda asked.

"I recall seeing Brandy go inside. After about fifteen minutes, the rest of the party, around twenty people, all left in a mass exit. It was something."

"How do you know that?"

"Well, because everyone jumped in their cars and took off. It was like some mass exodus, as I said."

Glenda nodded. "So you're thinking that he pretty much has a hold over her?"

"I know he used to. But you see, that was when he cared. He's made it really clear he doesn't care about Brandy any more. In fact..." she didn't finish.

"What?"

"I shouldn't say this."

The restaurant lights had been lowered. The room had cleared out somewhat. Now the bags under Jan's eyes were visible. Her cropped hair was coming out of its barrettes.

"It's just that for a long time I thought Brandy would end up being a statistic."

"As in, murdered?"

She nodded. Her pupils were black and dilated. "I think the only reason Brandy has survived is because she's Charlie's mother." She stared at nothing. Her voice was contemplative.

"You can't be serious. You think he'd go so far as to murder her? It sounds like she's annoying, but beyond that—what has she done to him?"

Jan's eyes narrowed. "There's always been something about the Saxony family, at least that's what I've come to learn. There is a bizarre energy. And Brandy is involved in some strange practices. They have argued out on the front lawn about her involvement in whatever it is."

Glenda looked around the room, recognizing a few friends from college. The owner of the place she knew as Brett. Rosedale had that flavor about it; for as much as people came and went, there persisted a familiar continuity. "I think we need to go to River Falls. It cannot be put off any longer. Is there anything else you can tell me about the Saxony family?"

"Well, Robby Saxony is your typical enduring misogynist. From what I understand, it seems to be a family trait passed on over the many generations of Saxony men."

"And," Glenda added, "not only is it a genetic trait, the behavior is passed on too. And especially, I would think, in a male-dominated business. But from all I've heard, there seems to have been something deeper, something more sinister prevalent in the Saxony family. Don't they have a history of odd or unexplained deaths in the family?"

"Yes." Jan's blue eyes were wide and intense. "But primarily with the women. Still, I didn't want to say anything when you told me about some items from the Saxony family that somehow landed at your shop."

Jan's eyes fluttered. A tear welled in her eyes.

"Jan, what are you talking about?"

"You're going to think I'm crazy."

"What?"

"It's been rumored around town, and believe it or not, by some other antique dealers, that items which have belonged to the Saxony family carry bad luck. Like cursed karma or something."

Glenda laughed as she added another creamer to her coffee. "You mean like a curse? Like King Tut? Aren't these just items from a family? From old family money or the family company?"

"They carry the evil with them," Jan said in a hoarse whisper.

By now, the late dinner crowd had cleared out. It neared 10 P.M.

"Can you tell me what some of the items are?" Jan asked carefully.

Glenda tinkered with the spoon next to her coffee cup. The waitress had her hand propped on her hip. She watched them. Glenda smiled and the woman brought over the pot of coffee.

"There is a camera that is quite interesting. The bottom of it is inscribed 'William Saxony.'"

"My God. How did you get that?"

"It was very strange. I guess Mindy went on a day of estate sales. But she said the camera wasn't from a Saxony estate sale. She claims that someone anonymously dropped the item off at this person's house. It was as if they knew there was going to be an estate sale, but they didn't want anyone to know. Mrs. Peacock over on Ridge Avenue had just died."

"I know that family," Jan said. "Even the person in charge of the sale couldn't recall who had left the stuff."

"It was anonymous." Glenda stopped. She watched Jan carefully. After a moment, she said. "You truly believe there's a strange supernatural aura about the Saxony family?"

Jan sipped her wine, then set the glass down, clutching the stem.

"It's not just the family. It's the effect the men have on the women. Not that the women were right to allow it, but in William's time, it was expected. And since then it's been like an insidious form of mental abuse. From what I heard, William Saxony willed his women to be a certain way. Fanny, his wife, was a typical pure and God-fearing Victorian woman."

Jan laughed shrilly and shook her head.

"But," she continued, "he was cruelly negligent about the working conditions of the women in his factory. This is the same factory where ten women died because of inadequate exits or fire escapes. Now the building is the corporate office. It was a horrible accident. And many people feel it could have been prevented. In fact, others claim it wasn't an accident at all."

Glenda was thoughtful, her hand to her chin. "Let's go to my store. I have to check on a few items."

"Sure," Jan agreed.

Leaving the restaurant, they walked along in the evening air. Jan finally spoke.

"Wasn't there a woman at the company William became involved with?"

"Two women. Eliza Mortimer and Penelope Rutherford."

"Yes. One of them was mixed up with an extreme woman's organization. It was an anti-suffragette movement."

"Anti-suffragette? That makes no sense if both Eliza and Penelope were working women." Glenda said.

"Apparently both were actually husband hunting. And whoever it was went right to the top. Unfortunately, Eliza fell for William, and fell very hard. He made her sad Victorian life even more insufferable. Conditions were bad enough for women. But William went further. First he seduced Eliza and then ruined her reputation. She was a naive farm girl who came to Chicago's North Shore purely by chance." Jan was quiet, then continued. "That's what strikes me about Robby," she said.

They'd reached In Retrospect. Glenda jiggled the skeleton key in an aged front door lock. "Yes?"

"Well, Robby's method of operation is to wheel in any new female employee, whoever she is, then break her down gradually. It's mental abuse; teasing and breaking down self-esteem. He especially works to demean their intelligence level and then he proceeds to their appearance."

"Interesting, look what I've found," Glenda said. She yanked on a box of albums. "Listen to this," she said, pulling out a small one with faded newspaper clippings in it. "Here is one from September 15, 1903. 'A Mr. William Saxony, president of Saxony Skirts in Northwoods, Illinois, is being investigated for the deaths of ten women who died in a factory fire last week. His behavior indicates that he blames the women themselves.'"

The telephone rang.

"In Retrospect, Glenda Morgan speaking."

"Yes. My name is Brandy Saxony. I need your antique expertise.

35

But it has to be completely confidential. And the merchandise is housed upstate in Illinois."

Glenda's mouth dropped open.

"That should be no problem," she said quickly. "Just give me directions to wherever the antiques are. It sounds simple enough."

A long pause. "No. That's just it. It's far from simple. It's somewhat dangerous."

Glenda looked at Sandy, her eyes narrowed. "How can that be?"

"Answer this," Brandy said breathlessly. "Do you believe in the supernatural?"

CHAPTER FOUR

Jan scanned the article while Glenda maneuvered the winding roads which led to River Falls.

"It says here that William Saxony 'practiced perpetual attention to details, perfection at tasks and promptness. The ten women who died in the factory fire included local women from Rosedale, Glen Ayre, and Northwoods, and even farther north like Lake Bluff and Waukegan. No further investigation into the fire is expected. It has been ruled an accident due to unfortunate carelessness.'"

"Can you believe that?" Glenda said. "Somehow William Saxony was able to blame the tragedy of ten deaths and his negligence about the condition of the factory and its inadequate exits on the women themselves. And the real gall is that they didn't even investigate the deaths."

"Now where exactly are we going? River Falls, but why there?"

"Believe it or not, Jan, I thought it would be good for you to have a couple days off after what's happened. Listen to this: I was looking over an old camera from the collection Mindy found at an estate sale. The name on this particular camera said William Saxony. And the weird thing is that the box of photographs I found with the camera included a number of pictures of a young woman—shot in many different poses. It's as if the woman had multiple personalities."

"Like a split personality?"

"Well, let's say a woman of many moods."

"Why are you so interested in this woman in particular?"

"I'll tell you why. She has something to do with the Saxony's. Read some more from this article to me."

Glenda handed her another article she'd stashed in the glove box.

"Let's see," Jan said. "William Saxony, respected president and founder of Saxony Skirts and Company in Northwoods, Illinois, was found slain in his executive offices. A Miss Eliza Mortimer has been taken into custody by police. Surrounded by a massive quantity of blood, Mr. Saxony's throat had been severed with a cut-throat.'"

"What is a cut-throat?" Jan asked. "It sounds gruesome." Glenda noticed that Jan was rubbing her hands together.

"And why is it so important," Jan continued, "that we investigate the history of the Saxony company?"

"For several reasons," Glenda said. "A cut-throat refers to a razor—the kind they used to use in the barber shops at the turn of the century. They were sharp and nasty. The second reason I think we should investigate the history of Saxony is that you said the victim, Elizabeth Marx, found at Saxony was wearing a Victorian costume. Some think the perpetrator may have dressed her that way."

"Yes," Jan answered. "And the only reason I heard that was because Sandy, in her capacity at her job, can hear just about every conversation Robby Saxony has both inside and outside his office. Someone was sending a message—to the police or the press or God knows who—a message about the Saxony company but even more about the Saxony family. What is the message? What are their dirty secrets? What brought this on?" Jan finished finally.

"It was those photographs I found with the camera, Jan, those numerous shots of a woman. She was dressed to look like Eliza Mortimer—she was wearing glasses in one and sitting in front of her typewriter in another. But it wasn't her—I swear. It was a woman dressed to look like her. And then I saw this."

She pulled a crumpled article out of her purse and handed it to Jan. "Look at the picture in this article and compare it to the group here."

Jan eyed the photograph—a smear of light grey circling the two characters, cloudy and faded. The eyes immediately captured the viewer. A woman in a dark dress and high button boots had her mouth set seriously. There was a trace of evil whimsy awaiting to break, but the eyes themselves were telling—wide and brown and clearly crazed.

"It's labeled 'Eliza Mortimer.' But this clearly isn't her," Jan said. "How could no one have seen that?"

"And now Brandy Saxony has commissioned us to go up and appraise some obscure items. I'm not sure about the place—this cottage or chalet. I think it was a love nest for William and Eliza. Brandy was pretty vague about the history."

"So this is a business trip?" Jan said, almost hopeful.

"You bet. What's great is it's lucrative and enigmatic. But seriously," Glenda said, eyeing Jan carefully. "Detective Halloran—you know, my friend on the force in Rosedale—he told me this was a nasty murder. He thinks this murder has the makings of a lunatic killer."

"A nasty murder," Jan repeated. "It's very unnerving."

"And it's all connected," Glenda said. "This untimely incident— Robby Saxony being spotted in his garage and then somehow, almost concurrently, the murder of his assistant. And it was as if the antiques from the Saxony family themselves came to us. As if they found us somehow. And then Brandy calls and orders me on this strange excursion up north."

Jan looked troubled. "I forget how big Illinois is until you really drive for a while, you know?" She let her voice trail away. "What's the name of this lodge? And why are the Saxony antiques there?"

"Here's the strange thing. It's all happening on the heels of this murder of Elizabeth Marx. Why is Brandy wanting her husband's family antiques appraised? Why now?"

"Unless," Jan said, looking thoughtful, "she's hiding something. Or maybe she knows something about the murder that needs to be revealed. I've always had a problem with Brandy Saxony, I'm sorry to say. She's a different breed from Robby. She's not of his caliber in a way. Even though he's a rat."

Glenda frowned and looked out the window. She sensed Jan's dislike of Brandy. Disapproval or jealousy? "How did they meet, do you know?"

"Robby and Brandy? Robby had a restaurant for a short time in Rosedale. Remember the Turntable Restaurant? Brandy worked there as a waitress. She charmed him somehow."

Glenda indeed sensed the ugly face of envy in there somewhere.

"Robby moved back to Glen Ayre right out of college. He started up at his father's company like a good prodigal son and then got the restaurant as something on the side. He really didn't know how to manage a restaurant though. His entrepreneurial attempts didn't last. So he licked his wounds back at Saxony."

"I see. So would you say it's been a stormy marriage?"

"To say the least," Jan said. "And when they moved in to their lovely monstrosity of a house, they started airing their dirty laundry on a daily basis." Jan looked out the window, at the light posts flipping past. In her lap, her hands were folded.

A peaceful image. A false image. Glenda knew Jan better than that.

"It's really upsetting you, isn't it?"

"What?"

"That you had to be a witness the night of the murder. And now with Sandy and her new position working directly for Robby, you're not sure how you feel about that, are you?"

Jan nodded, fighting tears. She bowed her head, covering her face with her hand. Jan had a small oval face and stood no more than five foot one. She had short blonde hair and pale blue eyes. Her camouflaging of tears struck Glenda as sad. She thought Jan might be teetering on the edge of a breakdown.

"Are you sure you're fine with this trip?" she asked her.

"I'll admit I'm a little worried about Sandy."

"Why don't we call her when we get to the cabin?"

"Yes, thanks, let's do that. What exactly is this place we're going to? What else did Brandy say?"

"I'm not sure what her status is in the Saxony family, but she's insistent about the antiques being appraised. And she wants it to be confidential. She said it's a lodge. But now that you mention it, she was very hesitant to talk about the rumors, which I know about. They say that the place has a history involving old William Saxony and that it's haunted, of all things. He used to cavort there with his mistress, Eliza Mortimer."

"What is it now? Is the lodge a rental property?"

"I don't know. I have a friend from college who stayed there last summer and she swears it's haunted." She shook her head. "I think we only have about ten miles left."

"It's getting really dark," Jan said. "The woods seem to be closing in on us."

Glenda nodded. "The trees are definitely taller. I love the pines." She squinted. "But now I can't see very well."

Suddenly she screeched to a stop. The sound of pavement gave way to gravel. She flicked on her brights. They were enveloped in black night and silence. "Someone is supposed to meet us here with the key to the cabin."

"Let's hope they remembered," Jan's voice was shaky.

"I'm sure he'll show," Glenda said.

"He has to show," Jan whispered.

The car closed in, the small space making Glenda feel trapped. She leaned over and reached for a flashlight from her glove compartment.

"I'm going to look around," Glenda said.

"Out there? Outside the car? In the dark?" Jan asked.

"Do you want to come with me?"

"Are you crazy?"

Glenda peered out the front windshield. The small chalet had a wide porch that wrapped all the way around, the roof slanting in a wide-hipped style typical of a turn of the century cottage bungalow. There were ribbons of wide windows all around the building. Clearly a place to enjoy the view. In daylight. At night, the view would be more harrowing.

"Glenda, I'll wait here."

Glenda opened her door. A sound. No lights—just a sound.

"I'm going to check it out," she said. "Who knows? Maybe he left the key under the mat."

"That would be really foolish," Jan said. "It doesn't look friendly around here."

"I don't know how to remind you of this," Glenda said, "but we're sleeping here tonight. In this cabin."

"Here?"

"I'm sorry. I thought you knew."

"You told me. I guess I put it out of my mind."

Glenda walked off then, shining her flashlight straight up to the little cottage. She ascended the stairs and stepped onto the wrap-around porch. She went right to the door. There was something ominous and dark about the place. The floor creaked. There was peeling paint on the door. It had a bulbous brown doorknob. She jiggled it. Then she spotted a note taped next to it. "Key is under the mat." High security in a small town, she thought.

Kneeling, she reached for the mat. As she did so, it seemed to move. She grabbed it then with both hands and lifted it up. Finding the key, she raced down the stairs and back to the car.

Standing at the passenger side window, she shined the flashlight. But she was unable to see Jan. Her stomach felt sick. Jan was not in the car.

She turned in a circle. "Jan!" she called out.

Then she heard a sound of crushing leaves and a shrill cry from behind her. She whipped around again and again, shining the flashlight wildly. Then silence. She could hear the lapping of the lake somewhere nearby.

Finally she looked back to the house. Did her eyes deceive her? A floating image lingered there on the porch, the wind seeming to tug at it, stretching it back and forth. The longer Glenda stared at the apparition, her eyes watering from the cold, the more it took on shape. Could she see feet? There was a long flowing dress and a lacy high collar and hair tied up in a bun. But the vision's feet didn't touch the ground but rather seemed to scrape the floor.

Glenda blinked, wiping her eyes to see more clearly. Instantly what she thought she saw dissipated. An elongated white form stretched before her. Then a deafening scream.

"Glenda!"

Glenda raced back to the foot of the stairs, her heart a manic flutter. She heard heavy steps running around the porch. Then Jan fell at Glenda's feet. Glenda leaned down and helped her up, dropping her flashlight. The light went out and she heard something rolling.

"Where were you? What happened? Why did you leave the car?"

"You told me to come over right away."

"No I didn't. Did you seen anyone?"

"See anyone?"

Glenda groped around on the floor, searching for the flashlight. "I've dropped the flashlight and the battery rolled somewhere. But I did find the key." She was out of breath.

"Glenda, I'm scared. Are you all right?"

"Let's just get our stuff and go inside."

Within five minutes they'd hauled and thrown down several duffel bags inside the rustic log cabin. Glenda finally found one small kerosene-style lamp that lit.

"How can anyone see where they're going in this place?" Glenda said, turning around and jumping at her reflection in the half light of a tarnished mirror. The image was contorted. Was she just tired?

"Glenda?" Jan murmured. "You look very strange."

Glenda felt along the wall, her hands passing over an ornate sconce on the wall where crystal shades jutted out from long bronze fixtures.

"What are you looking for?"

"Matches. I just ran out." Then she remembered. "Wait, I have a lighter in my coat." Reaching into the pockets of her jacket she'd thrown over a chair, she found a small red lighter. Then she walked to the first sconce and lit something white inside of it. It came to life.

"Gas lighting?" Jan said. "Why would that be?"

"Part of the charm of the place I'm sure," Glenda said, turning around, hand to her chin. Then she started at something and realized it was her own reflection in the mirror again. Then the lights went out, all except the lantern.

"It feels warm enough too," Jan said.

"The caretaker of the place is a crusty old man named Joe Brown. He said he'd warm the place up for us ahead of time. He did not tell me about the gas lighting surprise though."

Glenda circled the room. The floor consisted of wide planks and was covered by a mammoth oriental rug. Along the windows were wicker rocking chairs. On the walls were the earthy decorations crafted a century earlier; Victorian hair braided designs placed under glass and several designs comprised of flowers. The wallpaper was an intricate weaving of woodland leaf patterns.

Glenda took a deep breath. The place smelled of pine trees and damp wood. She had always liked that smell. It reminded her of childhood camp trips.

"Unique little fixtures and additions they have here," she said.

Glenda collapsed in a wicker chair, feeling the first wave of weariness from the drive up. "And the wicker furniture," she said, letting her voice trail away. "It's very authentic."

Jan paced around the room, circling a table with four chairs placed in the center of the room. Around and around she walked, studying the design of the oriental rug beneath the set.

"There are two single beds in a small bedroom in the back. It's really a cozy little place."

Glenda tried to hide the tremor in her voice. She hated to admit that she felt daunted by the initial investigation of the place. She yawned. "Why am I so tired all of a sudden?" Glenda said.

"What was that?" Jan said, becoming panicky.

"What?"

But Glenda too felt her stomach jump. She'd heard something. A

43

scratching swishing sound.

"It's an animal. You know how these raccoons ransack these little places."

Yet even as she spoke, Glenda struggled to believe her own words. Jan continued to circle the table, around and around.

"Jan. You're making me dizzy, for God's sake."

"What's the matter, Glenda?" Jan blurted. "Do you sense something wrong about this place?"

Glenda stood up and walked briskly to view several large photographs arranged around the mirror. Immediately she was drawn to the first one. It was a photo of a young woman. She was small in stature and wore a long white dress with layers of ruffles draped around the bottom and some ruffles at the cuffs. The overall impression was that of a simple dress without a lot of decoration or adornment. She wore wire-rimmed glasses and a confident grin. One of her hands was propped on her hip.

"This is certainly not typical of those days," Glenda said.

Jan walked over slowly. "What do you mean?"

"She's wearing her glasses, for one. And the way she is standing—with so much bravado. I like her gusto."

"Maybe this was a brothel. She could be a prostitute."

"Jan," Glenda said, "why would you say that?"

Even as Glenda spoke, a foreign presence seeped in, as if making her cold all at once. She tried to focus on the photo but it somehow blurred, and then cleared. That's when she deciphered the name scrawled at the bottom.

"'To William, affectionately, Eliza.' This must be Eliza Mortimer."

"Eliza?"

"She was accused of murdering William Saxony, remember? A brutal murder too," she said, then forgetting Jan's timidity. "I told you, they called her 'Eliza the Slasher.'"

"Stop it, Glenda," Jan said, sitting up in the chair and looking around. "Just stop it already."

"I'm sorry," Glenda said, but suddenly she felt even more tired. She plopped into a chair located next to Jan. Glenda was at a loss as to what to say. She knew Jan was spooked but there was so much to be talked about and figured out. Jan looked up slowly.

"What do you mean she was a 'slasher'?"

"I thought you didn't want to hear."

"Tell me," Jan said, urgently now, pulling out a bottle of Rolaids antacids.

"She used one of those cut-throats, you know," Glenda said slowly, watching Jan chew the tablets. "What the barbers used. And I'm sure this is Eliza not only because of the signature but because I found a file folder of pictures. Remember? With that camera from the Saxony stash. Mindy said that she had found it soon after the items amazingly appeared at In Retrospect. But this murder was brutal. I don't know a lot about the details but from what I've looked into, it sounded highly suspicious. And from reading about Eliza, I don't envy her. All she wanted was to move up in the company, but the men didn't like it. As a 'typewriter' she took a man's job, for starters."

Again, Glenda's voice trailed off. "And the proof was circumstantial. I want to find out more while we're here. She was the last person seen with him. That was it. But she worked for him."

"But why here?" Jan said, sounding angry all at once.

"What is it, Jan? We're here to look at the antique items. And if we find out anything else, I'm all for it. We both want to find out as much as we can about the Saxony family, don't we?"

"You're right. I'm sorry," Jan said, fighting tears. "I'm just overwhelmed. And I'm worried about Sandy."

"Why don't you call her again?"

Jan stood up and walked to the old rotary phone. She lifted the red receiver. "It's actually connected? This place is so creepy I was sure this would be a dead line. You know, something out of a horror movie."

Glenda smiled. Jan turned, phone receiver to her ear. Glenda's mouth was open. Her eyes were wide.

"What is it?" Jan said.

Glenda leaned on the table to support herself. Then she pointed beyond where Jan stood, unable to speak.

CHAPTER FIVE

All had gone black. Nothing. No sound. Just a wisp and sudden cold. Suddenly the gas light sconces flickered on and off three times. Glenda thought she saw a chair slide across the room.

Glenda lowered her arm slowly. She felt a cold hand on hers, firmly resting upon her own, and she recoiled.

"Jan?" she said. "Where are you?"

"What are you doing?" Jan said.

"I'm here," Glenda replied, her voice thin and raspy. "I thought I saw something. Or felt something."

"What happened to the lights?" Jan said, sounding panicky. "The lights! The damn lights!"

"It was probably a power outage," Glenda said. "It's an old cabin."

As she said this, a little lamp flickered on. Glenda had relit the Colman gas lantern hanging on the wall. "Look," Glenda said, "we're both tired. Let's just unpack and have some tea or something. Isn't that what you do to calm down at these cabins? I brought a picnic dinner and some sodas too. How's that sound?"

"Great."

Jan threw her small overnight bag on the floor of the diminutive bedroom. Glenda wandered around the cabin, cutting through the dim light gently. A soft feeling followed her to another door. This door was situated behind a wicker chair as if hidden there. Why would the chair be placed there? On purpose? It was as if to draw attention away from the door.

"This is weird," she said quietly.

"What?" Jan said, rushing in from the other room.

"Nothing. It looks like there's a room here that's locked." The lights flickered and brightened again. "I wonder where this Joseph person is. He was supposed to meet us."

"What do you mean? Like something happened to him?"

"I don't know."

Half an hour later, the two women finished up dinner and retired with books to bed.

The following morning there was a heavy knock on the cabin door. Both women sat up in their beds simultaneously.

"My God, who is that?" Jan said, pulling the covers up.

"It's probably just that Joseph guy."

Glenda threw on her faded DePaul sweatshirt and her jeans and padded to the door.

"Hello," she said through the screen door to a smallish man with an aged face, the face of an old man in a barbershop. In a flash Glenda felt oddly transported to another time period somehow. The man mirrored the cabin in his mysterious antiquity. A matched set.

"I'm Joseph. Sorry I wasn't here to meet you proper yesterday. You want those antiques you come to look at? Some Brandy Sacks called me up bright and early this morning."

"Brandy Saxony," Glenda said, shaking her head. "She's certainly keeping tabs on us," she muttered.

Jan crept up behind her. "Who is it?" She pulled her bathrobe around her tightly.

"This is Joseph," Glenda said. She turned back to face him. She should probably ask him in for coffee. But there was something amiss about him.

"I won't bother you ladies."

"Please," Jan blurted, "we'd like to be done with our work today. Right, Glenda?"

Glenda nodded. "Come in, please."

Joseph walked in and Glenda plugged in her portable pot she'd brought along. "I wanted to ask you," she said. "Why do you have gas lighting in this old place?"

Joseph frowned, his face pained by the question. "What do you mean?"

"Right here," Glenda said, grinning, reaching over to the first sconce, amused by William Saxony's decorative touch. She examined it but found no paraffin inside. She walked along, checking the other sconces.

"I'm afraid, Miss," he said, "the only light we have is that little one. I been meaning to get some more lights in here. If you stay another night I can try to dig one up."

"No way!" Jan blurted.

Both Joseph and Glenda turned.

"I mean, I can't stay here again. I have so much work waiting. I run a graphics arts studio from my home and I have a ton of clients calling me. I mentioned all my business to you Glenda, didn't I?"

"Of course, Jan, I understand." Then she turned to Joseph. "I need to transport these antiques back to Rosedale. Did someone from the Saxony family tell you?"

Joseph hesitated, his hand to his grizzled chin. "I don't know about that, Miss. No one from the Saxony camp has told me anything. You know how that goes."

"That's fine. I'll return Brandy's call."

The coffee dripped slowly, making a soothing early morning sound; it was the organic calm of running water. The aroma filled Glenda's nostrils, providing some amount of courage to face the Saxony lot.

"Hello, may I speak with Brandy Saxony? This is Glenda Morgan calling from River Falls."

"This is Sestina. Hold, please."

Glenda waited.

"Hello? Glenda Morgan? You're the antique lady, right? This is Brandy."

"You phoned me?"

"It is important that the items you look over for me stay confidential. In particular, exactly what each item is that you find. And I'd like you to drive the items back with you."

"That's no problem."

"Also, keep the items well stashed away when you get home."

"Of course. I'll store them at my shop. I have a back room. Are you expecting any odd items in particular that you want me to look out for?"

Brandy didn't answer right away. "Let's just say these items have long been under wraps by Amanda Saxony. Look, can I tell you something just between you and me?"

"Of course," Glenda said, pacing around, fiddling with the cord.

Joseph stood looking out a picture window that faced the lake. He jingled change in his pockets which was annoying Glenda. Jan paced, spilling small drops of steaming coffee. She'd put on overalls and a sweater. Then Joseph eyed Glenda carefully, as if trying to figure out what the person at the other end of the phone was saying.

Glenda hung up the phone. "Interesting," she said simply.

"Have a cup of coffee, Glenda," Jan said. "Shouldn't you get dressed? I mean, we have to get moving and look over the stuff."

Glenda nodded. She turned to Joseph. "What can you tell me about this cabin? Who did it belong to?"

Joseph's eyes widened. "You're kidding me, right? Aren't you tight with those Saxony people? If not, then I can tell you the real skinny on those rich folk."

Glenda shook her head. "I don't know them personally. My friend Jan does to a degree. But we'd appreciate it if you would tell us what you know."

"Come on," he said, limping to the locked door. "I'll get you started."

He worked the key and soon finessed it open. "My God," he said, "shocks me every time."

Glenda too stepped back a moment. The first antique to catch her eye was a tall hat rack and next to it, a foyer wardrobe closet. She entered the room slowly, passing by a sewing bust—an old sewing machine and a victrola in one corner.

"Did this Brandy Saxony explain to you what this little love nest was all about?" he asked.

Glenda shook her head. Kneeling, she opened a large steamer trunk and pulled out white frilly negligees circa 1900.

"This was the place where old William Saxony brought his favorite mistress. I'm sure you saw the pictures in the main room. The lovely Eliza Mortimer turned heads in the early 1900s. Yes, little Miss Eliza the Slasher. They say her ghost hangs round the place. And then there was that Penelope Rutherford woman too."

"What?" Jan said, startled.

"Here?" Glenda asked.

"Yes," he said chortling. "But it's Eliza's ghost all right."

"Penelope Rutherford was involved with William Saxony too."

"Suppose so," he said. "Most of that gossip was kept secret, though. The Rutherford woman had money."

Glenda nodded. Jan paced even more.

"Yes, but that Eliza the Slasher. She was no slasher like they accused her. And then there was the whole scandal about one of his mistresses being pregnant. Anyway, have a look here in the room," he said, waving his hands.

"Brandy instructed me to bring back everything. I'm not to leave anything behind."

"Good luck, ladies. You should know, Miss Eliza the Slasher may make a visit now and again."

"What?" Jan said again, clearly alarmed.

"They say she come back in 1923. And then there was a rash of more murders at that same time. No one really knew much about Miss Molly Mortimer. She was the second woman calling herself Mortimer. But no one ever forgot her, I'll tell you."

"Who was Molly Mortimer?" Glenda asked.

"Some say Molly Mortimer was actually Eliza. Slasher Eliza coming back to get her vengeance on the Saxony company for her wrongful hanging. She was not resting in peace, as they say."

Glenda nodded, looking thoughtful. Then she glanced at Jan. Jan's face had gone white and her whole body seemed to convulse.

"What's the matter?"

"Nothing. Let's just get through this."

Glenda nodded at Joseph and then stepped over and spoke softly to Jan. "It's going to take a little longer than I thought. But Brandy insists that we assess this stuff while we're still up here. I've brought my catalogs."

Jan shook her head. "I can't do it. I just don't know. I feel very strange."

Her voice bordered on hysteria. Joseph had stepped back by the front door.

"I'll be going now, Miss," Joseph said. "Let me know what you need. There's a little place in town down the road where you can grab some meals."

"Thanks, Joseph," Glenda said.

Glenda led Jan into the room with the four chairs situated around the table. "Take a seat," she said, helping her into a chair. "What is it?"

"That room. It feels so full. I can't explain. Almost heavy or stuffy."

Suddenly there was a clicking sound, as if a light switch were

51

being turned on and off. Both women stopped talking. It grew colder in the cabin all at once. The light flickered. Glenda stood up.

"Let's go outside and get some sun with our coffee. It's not good staying in here and getting spooked."

Jan followed Glenda out onto the wide wrap-around porch. The air was a freshly washed clear breath of trees, wood, and moisture. They walked to the side of the house and both took deep breaths. In all directions pine trees swayed directly in front of a clear lake. It was uninhabited. There were no other houses around it. Glenda counted only two chalets across the lake.

"It is beautiful," Jan said, then sipped her coffee. Her face still had an alabaster pallor about it.

"We really need to get going on the antiques. I'll go in and get started."

"What can I do?"

"Well," Glenda said, stepping back inside the cabin, "if you would pull the items out of boxes and clean them up a little, then I can have a look at them. I'm only giving Brandy a rough idea of what's here. I informed her that the accurate appraisals I'd have to do from my office."

actual?

"You still think it will take until..." Jan hesitated, following Glenda into the spare room... "tomorrow?"

Glenda nodded. "But Jan, if you need to, I can put you on a comfortable bus home this afternoon."

"No, I'll be fine."

An hour passed. Glenda had dusted off the coat and hat racks, the ornate oak wardrobe, and the cherry wood victrola. She pulled up a small bench and sat next to a large wooden box. Lifting the lid she found a stereoscope. Accompanying it were two leather-bound boxes of double imprint photographs—the same photo appeared on the left and right of each thick piece of cardboard.

"What are those?" Jan asked.

"This is called a stereoscope," Glenda said. "It was an early method of viewing photographs. You look through this part here," she said, holding the stereoscope by the handle, then looking through a headpiece for the eyes. She placed one of the cardboard photographs in the top of the device. "And then the two pictures combine to look like one three-dimensional photo, sort of."

Jan took the item from Glenda and held it, looking through the goggle-type piece on top of the thing. "Interesting," she said.

Glenda flipped through the photos in the first box. On the side, the box was identified as "Saxony family photos." "Must have been a rich family," Glenda said, "to afford stereoscope photographs."

She flipped through several boxes of smiling family photos. One shot in particular showed a large group of women. They all wore similarly modest dresses according to the times. The women smiled, albeit guarded smiles, and behind them stood a tall man with a flamboyant mustache and cocky grin. He had his arms crossed over his chest. This particular photo had handwriting across it in silver ink which read, "William Saxony and the women of the factory."

"This one is quite a find," Glenda said. "What do you know about the Saxony history?"

Jan nodded. She looked uncomfortable. "It's a known fact that ten women died inside the Saxony factory in the fire-the very loft where Robby has his main offices now. It was back in 1903."

"The place was improperly equipped—without enough fire escapes," Glenda said..

"That was true. But there was even more from what I heard."

"It sounds like the Triangle Shirtwaist Factory fire in New York. Remember that? It was 1911. The place employed mostly women and children. They worked long hours in an unheated building and filthy conditions. Once the flames started, some workers suffocated, others jumped to their deaths. It turned out after the fire, they found out there were inadequate fire escapes and the doors opened inwards. Most were even kept locked. I think 143 women and girls died as well as three men."

"It was equally bad, and in some ways worse," Jan conceded, "even though it was a smaller factory and there were only ten deaths."

"Yes, I heard," Glenda said, "that the deaths were even more despicable because all the women were working late. Many of them were trying to move up in the company just to the starter positions of many of the men. The women labored at machines which were dangerous and outdated. Bobbins often broke. There were a lot of injuries. And like any factory, sometimes fingers were severed. But I heard the worst aspect of these deaths was that these same women had enjoyed picnics at the Saxony house over the years. One woman in particular was performing her usual sexual duties with Mr. William Saxony. He escaped. She didn't."

"What a swine," Jan said. "It goes back all the way, doesn't it?" *a long*

Glenda grinned.

"The whole male domination thing you mean?"

"Yes," Jan said, with much less humor than Glenda.

Glenda opened a drawer in a rolltop desk. "Jan, there's at least a half day's work here for tomorrow."

Jan shook her head. "Glenda, I've changed my mind. I cannot stay. Will you be all right here alone?"

Glenda picked through smaller items in the drawer, cards, marbles, some letters. In actuality, she was hesitant to stay in this bizarre cabin alone. But she simply nodded and continued to look through the stereoscope cards. Flashing through the last few cards she stopped, her eyes intent upon one of them.

"Well now, this is strange," she said.

"What?" Jan said, already visibly shaken.

"Look at this card. All the photographs on either side should be the same in order to work in the stereoscope. But the photo on the right here is of another woman—from the looks of it, a very troubled woman."

She handed the photo to Jan, whose eyes were wide. "She does look crazed," Jan agreed. "And the name here reads Penelope Rutherford. I wonder what her job was? Assistant? Seamstress? And some of these photographs I'm finding in here are pretty racy. I'll bet the activities with William Saxony included special photography sessions."

By late afternoon, both of the women were rummaging through the items mechanically, noting them in a log, after which Glenda reviewed them in more detail.

A sudden knock on the door made both the women start.

"I'm so sorry, ladies," Joseph said, appearing in a blur through the screen door.

His form gave out a menacing silhouette. There was minimal light in the room where the antiques were stored. All the sunlight from behind him beamed through the bungalow windows, wrapping around the front of the place.

"Look Joseph," Glenda said, stepping up, holding the stereoscope box. "Whom would I talk to for the local history of this place?"

Joseph shook his head. "Well, there's the local historical society.

It's over on Main and Second. Right in the heart of River Falls."

Glenda nodded, refilling her coffee cup. "No. What I need is the real dirt. I want gossip about the Saxony family, all about the factory fire and the photography that William Saxony was notorious for. That kind of information."

Joseph pulled a chair around the table and sat down. "That would be Dodie Carmichael. She's a bit of the old salt round here. She knew the Saxony family very well. She's got a lot of the inside knowledge."

"That's whom I need to see," Glenda said. "Thanks Joseph."

"One other thing," Glenda added, pressing for more. "Do you know if William Saxony was known for taking unusual photographs while visiting this little retreat? I know he brought women out here."

Joseph's brow furrowed. "Yes, I believe he did. I know there's a lot of photo equipment around."

"Yes, there is." Then turning to Jan. "The light outside is going, Jan. Let me get you on that bus."

The two women drove in silence to the bus station. Her small Volvo sputtered as she switched gears. Jan was immobile, her hands clasped together tightly on her lap. From a distance, the train station appeared deserted except for two figures. The car neared, its rattling seeming to break into a sacred silence. Suddenly as they drew closer, the two figures merged to only one. That of a woman.

"Look at her," Glenda said to Jan.

"At whom?"

Then they were very close. Glenda could discern the face clearly, even in the half-light of dusk. It was the face they'd identified as Penelope Rutherford. It was the same crazed visage wearing Victorian clothing.

"I see her," Jan murmured.

And just as quickly, the specter disappeared.

55

CHAPTER SIX

The backdrop was white. Glenda could make out an approaching figure, slim in a black dress and a white high-collared blouse. She walked swiftly, with intention. Then she hesitated beneath an elm tree. Glenda felt a need to talk to her but the woman seemed to be hiding something behind her back.

Suddenly there was screaming—loud and shrill—which carried beyond the expanse of grass to a mud patch around the tree.

Glenda whipped around and saw behind her the small Saxony factory. Although she could see numerous arms flailing in the windows and the sounds of screams kept on coming, her feet were planted. She couldn't move.

Turning around, she glanced back at the young woman in a black dress. She flowed past Glenda without pausing in her stride. All at once, a man stood by the tree, blocking something. He looked smug, his arms crossed over his chest. He wore a cocky grin. When Glenda looked at him, he tipped his hat to her.

"Why did you do that?" she wanted to say, but didn't. Somehow Glenda's voice wouldn't come. She wanted to slap his self-satisfied expression away as he stood there, so cavalier. His smile widened as he moved away from the tree, plodding toward her. Simultaneously, Glenda could see a woman in white wearing glasses. She was swinging in a large swing with floral-covered ropes.

Now she could see the woman wearing black, very close up. Her eyes were asymmetrical and intense, and her mouth wore a twisted grin. Suddenly it was raining. Her bangs lay flat and wet against her forehead. She regarded Glenda and broke into an uproar of laughter.

"You are Penelope Rutherford," Glenda said.

But the woman merely laughed.

Glenda sat up in bed suddenly, panting. The room was still and dark. She was completely alone. The dream had consumed her.

She peered around the room and was afraid of what she would see. Groping for her glasses by the bedside, she put them on.

Rolling out of bed, she marched through the main room to the front porch and took a deep breath of the night air. It was moist and crisp, as if autumn had hurried into being. A familiar cry of a cardinal took her back thirty years to childhood in Rosedale.

Then she heard something less familiar. But more recent. A woman's laughter came from without. She whipped to the right and backed up against the wall. The laughter intensified. She raced back into the cabin and flipped through her duffel bag to find her walkman radio. She checked her watch. 4:30 A.M. She would subdue her fear with Beethoven and pray for an early sunrise.

Two hours later, Glenda awakened on her stomach on the floor in the middle of the room. She stretched her arms above her head and looked around. That's when she noticed the shelf for the first time. It was small and seemingly insignificant but there it was. It was a small shelf located just above and to the left of the fireplace.

Shuffling to her feet, she strolled over to the shelf. She pulled down two books from the shelf—one was *A Pictorial History* of the United States and the other appeared to be a very old yearbook.

Always amused by the language and morals in older books, she flipped open the first one and a packet of letters dropped to the floor. As she bent to retrieve them, a loud knock sounded on the door.

"Yes?"

"It's Joseph."

She straightened up and pulled down her sweatshirt, opened the door, and let him in.

"I should be done by noon," she said. "Is that okay?"

Joseph looked at her, one of his eyes bigger than the other — asymmetrical and myopic, she thought, like Penelope Rutherford. As usual, he wore a baseball cap and overalls. Today he sported two flannel shirts, one under the denim and one over it.

"I thought I would visit Dodie Carmichael," she said. "Do you have her address?"

"You won't need it. She lives a mile down at the end of this road on the left corner."

Glenda was thoughtful. "What else do you know about Penelope Rutherford? Anything you haven't told me?"

He blanched. "Why would you ask me that?" he demanded.

Glenda was tired. The night had wrecked her emotionally and physically. And the dream...the dream about Penelope Rutherford. It was more than a dream. It was a message.

"I just need to know about her."

Joseph removed his baseball cap and scratched his head. "You can handle her. I'm sure of it."

"Excuse me?"

"Go see Dodie Carmichael. I'm not going to warn you. Just forget it. Forget it all!"

With that, he stormed out of the cabin and clomped down the stairs. Glenda followed him out onto the porch. The resonance of the heavy footsteps trailed off immediately and she was left with the deceptive calm of morning—the distant chirps of insects and birds indistinguishable, but still musical.

Showered and ready within half an hour, Glenda set out on foot for Dodie Carmichael's. Nearing the corner, however, she saw houses on three of the corners but the one to the left, kitty-corner as Joseph had said, was nothing but an old church. Oddly, it was painted bright red. It did not look to be in use.

Then she saw the address—51 Church Street.

She stepped across the street with a fluttery stomach and even more uncertainty. Standing at the front doors, she noted that they arched like those on a church. Something about this place was missing, however. She'd not yet figured it out. A lace curtain fluttered to the right, quickly, imperceptibly. But she knew for certain someone had checked her out. She knocked.

The sounds of numerous locks, and a key working the last of them, came from inside. She swung the door wide. There stood a small but powerful presence; something about her eyes was familiar and, at this early hour, very frightening.

"I'm sorry to call so early," Glenda said. "I need to talk to Dodie Carmichael."

"What about, for God's sake? Who are you, woman? No one comes to see me, ever."

Her voice was powerful for a small frame. Her words were enunciated clearly and with forethought.

"Joseph said you could tell me something about the Saxony

family. You know," she said, pointing behind her, "the man who once owned that cabin up the street?"

"I know what I know. What I don't know is if you're able to hear what I have to say. Most people around here deny what I say is true. They think I'm crazy. Who is this Joseph person, anyway?"

Glenda smiled ruefully. "I'm afraid I don't even know his last name. He just told me to see you."

The woman stepped back. "Come in. It's your risk."

Glenda noted with interest the woman's clothing. She wore a white dress with lace scallops at the hem, with two layers of fabric reaching to her ankles. Her blousy bodice matched the skirt and she wore four or five strands of different length pearls. Her thinning hair was swept up on top of her head, pulled together with pearl inlaid combs.

Glenda followed the woman into what appeared to be a great room—long and vast and lined with bookshelves on all sides. In the center of the room was one oblong table. It was draped with lace and numerous oversized books, some lying open to colorful illustrations and others just tossed about the table. In the center and slightly elevated on a small stand was a gold and blue crucifix.

Glenda cleared her throat. Dodie turned to look at her. Her expression was brazen.

"This is a unique house you have here."

Dodie glared. "It's my home," she said.

Spotting something in her peripheral vision, Glenda turned quickly, thinking she'd seen a shadow of someone moving to her left. It was only another set of doors that led into a smaller room. Dodie had decorated it like a provincial parlor.

"Please come in here," Dodie said, leading the way to a side room. "I'm not sure what I can tell you. I know everything. But I don't know what I should tell you. There's a difference, you see."

Scurrying steps sounded overhead. Glenda looked up. When she looked back at Dodie, the older woman hadn't moved.

"The evil began with William Saxony. He was a typical man. I heard of him only through word of mouth from my grandmother. He's the one who started it all."

Glenda studied Dodie a moment, the white layers of lace, the blue tint in her fine hair.

"Started it and ended it all. That's why she killed him."

Glenda sat up. "The slasher? Eliza Mortimer?"

Dodie frowned. "Eliza was not the murderer. Nor the slasher."

"I need to learn what you know about the Saxony Clothiers Company. You have to tell me."

Dodie's eyes narrowed. "Familiar with the history? I know the messes of that family! William Saxony had a sadistic hold over the town of Northwoods. At that time, we were just a tiny village. Then he came in and started the factory. It was around 1900 I would say. He had a claw-like hold on the town. We all knew the factory would help alleviate the poor financial situation of the town. And everyone was so surprised when he offered jobs to women."

"Your grandmother told you all that?"

"You just mind these words, young woman. What a shocker it was when Miss Eliza Mortimer started at the firm as a typewriter."

"A typewriter?"

"In those days, if you worked as a typist on a typewriter you were literally called a 'typewriter.'"

"Yes, I know," Glenda said, aware now that her slow comprehension annoyed Dodie Carmichael.

"Of course Mr. William Saxony came off looking like a hero. At first, that is."

Settled in a plushy tapestry-covered armchair, Glenda crossed her legs slowly.

Dodie sighed huffily. Suddenly scratching sounds came from overhead, then several thumps. Glenda started. Dodie just stared at her, unblinking.

"I suppose you want a cup of tea or a shot of bourbon or something?" she said.

Glenda stifled a laugh. "Tea would be nice."

The room had grown thin somehow, suddenly cold. Dodie stood up with a reluctant shuffle. Glenda searched the room, noting a pervasive scent that was spreading, replete with dust and old books. Glenda was reminded of the old barns and run-down shacks of her youth that were supposed to sell antiques. Often on car trips with her family, while driving through the prairie lands of Illinois and Wisconsin, she would beg her father to pull over at every sight, even the most dilapidated barn, which even mentioned antiques. Most of them carried the same odor, as if one life had been laid upon another

Heather!

and was now aging, thinning, and eroding, like the pages of books.

Glenda stood up and paced, examining a row of archaic photographs on the wall. Some were aged, black and white blendings, and pale. One depicted a group of women in a row, another showed just one woman. But what a woman. She recognized Eliza Mortimer in one, wearing the glasses and a determined grin. And this was the one they called 'the slasher.'

"That's her," Dodie said, placing chewing tobacco in the corner of her mouth. "The accused."

She set down the cup and saucer on a small table with a clatter.

"Isn't that tobacco hard on your gums?" Glenda asked.

"They had an exorcism, you know. Right here in the church."

"Excuse me?"

Glenda circled back to the chair and, as she sat, her eyes studied the older woman.

"Everyone in town knew that the real killer was the much beloved Penelope Rutherford. But you see, Penelope came from good stock, old family money. So no matter what the woman had done, everyone overlooked it. They tried to cure her of her homicidal tendencies right here in the basement of this old church."

"There was some sort of secret ritual, you mean?"

"Finish your damn tea and come with me," the old woman said, rising.

Glenda jumped up. As she followed, she had a sense of foreboding. She was overwhelmed by all the information that had been given to her. First Eliza Mortimer was accused of murder—but Penelope Rutherford was the killer. And now Brandy Saxony had insisted that Glenda go through all the Saxony antiques thoroughly. Was it for money? Were Robby and Brandy in financial trouble? Or was Brandy looking for something in particular? Something sinister in the Saxony past? She needed the elusive clue which would explain their maniacal tendencies. It was as if Brandy were plotting something and didn't want Robby or Amanda to know.

But now Glenda felt thoroughly immersed in the Saxony mire. And she had to admit, she'd always shivered at the thought of anything otherworldly or something she couldn't logically explain away. Again she heard the sounds from overhead—a scraping sound.

"Do you have raccoons or something?" she asked. No answer.

Soon they came to the end of a corridor and a flight of basement stairs.

"Now we will see the Saxony family for what they are. They didn't want the real murderer to be exposed you see."

"But wouldn't they want the killer to be punished?" Glenda asked. She thought of the savage eyes of Penelope and that photograph where she was out of place in the stereoscope. She reached into her pocket and pulled the photograph out. It was nothing, really. Simply paper and cardboard. Yet even as she held it in her hand, she felt life, the essence of Penelope Rutherford jump out at her.

Glenda trailed Dodie into the room and stopped at the sight of something monstrously large. Extending the length of the basement, where surely at one time the congregation had gathered for warm coffee cake and juice, there lay a steeple on its side, looking like a stricken soldier knocked breathless in battle.

"I want you to look around. Feel the place. I know you do already. There is an essence, isn't there?" Dodie's eyes were bright but shrewd. "Take a look around. Tell me what you glean from the remains of a horrific time."

Glenda's sense of discomfort hadn't subsided. In fact she felt a little sick, nauseous about the prospect of searching this dank basement for signs of the preternatural. As she walked around, she couldn't help but return to the steeple as it lay there, running the entire expanse of the room like some purple albatross. The very tip of the steeple jutted out into the hallway through a set of double doors.

"May I ask what a steeple is doing down here?"

A loud bell jingled. A rotary phone? Dodie scurried out to the hallway.

"Hello? Who? Glenda Morgan? Yes, she's here."

Who on earth would know she was here? This thought chilled her. Dodie stretched the red cord all the way into the vast room.

"It's for you," she said, her voice cracking.

"Hello?"

"Is this the woman from the Saxony cabin?"

"Yes. Of course."

"It's Joseph," he said gruffly.

"Yes?"

Slight hesitation, then he said, "Brandy Saxony called up. Wants you to call her right away."

Glenda frowned. "Thank you."

"Right away," he reiterated.

"Of course."

Glenda handed the receiver back to Dodie.

"May I make a call from your phone? I'm afraid it's long distance."

"Give me a dollar and go ahead."

Glenda pulled a small address book from her purse and looked under "clients" for Brandy and Robby Saxony's number. She dialed.

"Hello? Brandy Saxony, please. This is Glenda Morgan."

"Yes, Ms. Morgan. Thanks a lot for looking over the antiques. It's just that now I need you to bring them back to Northwoods right away."

"Your husband is probably anxious to see them, right?"

Glenda heard a quick intake of breath. "Absolutely not." Then she hesitated. "It's a surprise. I don't want Robby to know anything about these items. If you could just stow them at your store and I will meet you there. How much longer will you be?"

"We're finishing up." A lengthy silence. "We'll be seeing you soon."

"Who is 'we'?"

"I'm sorry, I mean, it's just me."

The two women ended the call. Dodie waited in the large room, hovering there, eavesdropping.

"Please, look around," she said.

"Am I looking for anything in particular?" Glenda asked.

"You'll find out."

Glenda didn't like this game. She walked around the room slowly, the mammoth steeple still staring her down. "Why is that here?" she blurted suddenly.

"It was no longer a church. After Penelope Rutherford's internment here, I'm afraid the negative energy she left gave me no choice. I feel the presence of the steeple is necessary."

Glenda strolled around. "The wallpaper is torn in numerous places," she said. "But it looks to be something beyond normal aging. In fact, it seems to be torn in some sort of pattern." She knelt down and ran her hand across the floor. "And there are numerous scuff marks on the floor. It's as if some battle went on here."

Dodie crossed her arms over her chest in her white dress of layers and lace. "Well, that's exactly what it was. Only my family would agree to live here after all the attempts to cleanse Penelope Rutherford and bring her back to sanity. She thought the wallpaper was alive, you see. There were little bugs crawling all over and there were all these exhortations to bring her around—she struggled quite a bit, scratching and kicking. I still have her black shoes with the little heels. They're upstairs. I keep them next to my bed. Would you like to see them?"

Glenda shook her head and side-stepped Dodie. She was aware that, for whatever reason, the older woman was trying to frighten her. Glenda held out the stereoscope card photograph she'd found which showed one picture as a family portrait and the other side the tormented face of a young woman.

"Is this Penelope Rutherford?"

"Yes." Dodie stepped back.

"It is not Eliza the Slasher?"

"No. And that woman who died, Elizabeth Marx? They found her in the ladies room. And only Robby Saxony was around. That was not just a murder."

"What?" Glenda was incredulous. "What do you know about that?"

"It was not just a murder, you see. It was a ritual."

CHAPTER SEVEN

Sandy Larson flipped through a pile of black and white photographs depicting cultivated women and arrogant-looking men. They were dropped in a pile brought back by Jan and Glenda from River Falls. She was careful to keep her hands and the photos tucked safely under her desk as she looked through them. An all- male executive team ran Saxony, except for Amanda Saxony. She hovered around Sandy's desk waiting to see Robby Saxony. According to the light on her telephone, Robby was still talking on a very serious phone call. He'd raised his voice several times.

"Does he know we're waiting?" Tom said from down the hall.

Sandy checked the light on the telephone and nodded without looking up. "He's still on the phone." She nodded at the light.

The man bristled. Amanda stalked up.

"What's going on here?" And without waiting, she barged into Robby's office and stood in front of his desk, her hands on her hips. "Robby? Some time today?"

"I have to go," he barked into the phone, slamming it down.

"Sandy," he said, storming over to her desk, "five copies. Two-sided." He tossed it on her desk, then whirled back into his office. Four other executives followed and the door was shut.

Sandy bit her lip and glared at the document. Picking it up, she slipped the photographs back into her center drawer, sliding a company envelope over them.

She kicked the copier when it jammed. Another assistant turned the corner. She was the head administrative assistant for the floor. She frowned. "That's not what you do."

"Whatever," Sandy said, grabbing her finished copies and plodding back to Robby's office. She tapped on his door, then walked in, in proper executive fashion, and set the copies on his desk.

Robby nodded, shooting her a loaded smile, following the lithe brunette with his eyes. Amanda slammed her hand on the table.

"Robby, tell us what you have from last week's meeting."

"Yes, Robby," the man Tom added. "I've had some trouble with orders not getting filled in production."

Sandy slipped out of the room. She knew the effect she was having on Robby. The realization made her cringe. Robby was a womanizer, a classic misogynist who only married a waitress just to annoy the patriarch Richard Saxony. The deal was marry now or lose your stock in the company. But in Sandy's mind, Amanda was really the scary one. Her motives seemed to seethe from deep inside, even where psychologists would fear to tread.

Back at her desk she reviewed the photos again. It was time to call Jan. The phone at Jan's house rang three, four times. She knew her friend had caller I.D. and often screened her calls. Jan would isolate herself especially during crippling bouts of depression. But surely she could see who it was calling? Unless she was in the shower. Sandy was about to hang up when an uneasy voice answered.

"Hello?"

"Jan? You don't sound like yourself."

"The bastard! He's such a bastard!"

"What's going on?"

"You don't know? Your boss just threatened me for over half an hour."

"That was you? About what?"

"He heard from the police. They're out to scare him, claiming that someone who had seen him in the garage now says he's not sure. And well, he figured out it was me. He threatened me, Sandy. Who was Elizabeth Marx? And why would he think I'd know anything?"

Sandy was quiet. "All I know about Elizabeth was that she was at one time a very strong-minded bright woman. She was going to law school, DePaul University I think, at night. And then she got messed up with Robby. I mean she had to know she wasn't the only woman he chased after. She was petite, pretty, with strawberry blonde hair."

"Just like his wife Brandy."

"In looks only. Believe me. But from what I've absorbed around the office, she broke it off with him. I think she was more interested in his business savvy, to be honest. That would be his knowledge about the workings of the company. She wanted to go into corporate law."

Jan sniffled at the other end of the line. "He said not only had he been watching my house but that he's hired thugs to make sure I stick to my story. He's threatening me, for God's sake!"

"I wonder what he's hiding? Either he is guilty in some way or he knows something. I know for sure he just wants this whole company mess to go away."

"But why is he going after me? What does he really think I know?"

"It is strange. Added to that, why did he suddenly transfer me over to work for him? I wonder if he knows you and I are friends."

Jan's crying slowed a bit. "Of course he knows," she said bitterly. "I've come into the office enough times to have lunch with you. In fact he said something about my being at the Christmas party he had a couple of years ago. Thought it was funny I was around so much. If I remember, though, his eyes were on you."

"Makes me sick actually. He doesn't realize that I'm going to find out everything I can. For instance, these pictures you gave me," Sandy said lowering her voice. "The one that interests me most is the stereoscope copy Glenda made for me. It's the one where the woman is on the right in a group shot of happy-looking people. Who the hell is she? One troubled-looking gal."

"Glenda knows about her. I couldn't take any more up at that cabin."

"What cabin? In River Falls?"

"Oh my God. That place. It unnerves me just to tell you about it. Glenda says she saw an image of a woman, something like a spirit. And late that night we heard noises and that was just too much. I couldn't take it. I had to leave. I left her there alone that night."

"Glenda? Sounds like a brave woman."

"We're going to a Monty Python double feature tonight at the Round Theater. Meet us there."

Sandy laughed. She realized she hadn't laughed all morning. "I love Monty Python but I'm sure Robby will have me working late, again."

"Making you work late? Business as usual, it sounds like."

"He's notorious for making his assistants work late."

"That's not all he's notorious for. I'd be careful if I were you."

69

Jan paused. "Besides. That's not all I wanted to tell you. I'm being stalked."

"What? By whom?"

Jan's voice started to quiver again. "I'm pretty sure it's Brandy Saxony."

"Brandy Saxony?"

"She's making no attempt to disguise her identity."

Sandy looked out the large picture window next to the closed door of Robby's office. Now late fall, the rolling greenery of the landscaped property was sprinkled with golden autumn leaves. Deceivingly serene. So much insanity in this little acorn of the North Shore.

"When have you noticed her?"

"I left to walk my dog Ruby at five o'clock this morning. I couldn't sleep. And there she was, wearing her little fur jacket. It was cool this morning. But I recognized her right away. She has that wild head of blonde hair, you know, several shades worth. I wanted to turn around and say something but when I'd stop, she'd stop. She wore sweat pants and a turtleneck, like she'd just thrown her clothes on and left the house in a hurry. And I know she has a dog but she wasn't even walking her. It's some sort of toy poodle. The thing has a diamond collar."

"That doesn't necessarily mean she's stalking you. What reason would she have to do that?"

"Who knows with the Saxonys? The whole family is obsessive. It could be that I saw her get home late that night she says she was out with friends. How do we know she didn't know all about Robby's little romps with Elizabeth Marx? Was that her name?"

"Yes. Look," Sandy said quickly. "I have to go. The meeting is closing up. Robby will probably want to see me."

"Call me later."

"I will." Sandy set the phone down gently.

She looked up placidly as the group filed out of Robby's office. Amanda explained something with exaggerated gesticulations, waving her hands as she spoke. Her executive colleagues listened. Some nodded, others checked their day planners.

"Sandy," Robby said firmly. "Come in now. We have a presentation due tomorrow."

Sandy grabbed a legal pad and followed him in. She sat in a

hardbacked chair opposite his desk and waited, pen poised. She looked past him out the window, her mind on the photographs and that odd woman in the one picture. Then she thought about Elizabeth Marx. Everyone in the office had been pretty shaken up by the murder, understandably. After days of questioning those who were known to be at the office which included only Robby, herself, and one other assistant named Kathy, the police had exhausted initial leads. Still, Sandy sensed the strange eyes upon her. And it didn't help that Robby had hired her away from her own boss right after his assistant had been strangled and killed.

"Where's your mind?" Robby interrupted her reverie. Then he sat back on the desk and continued in a new tone of voice. "Did you know in this light I can see just how blue your eyes are? Never noticed before now."

"Let's get to work on the proposal."

"Are you in a hurry? You agreed to work late whenever I need you, isn't that right?"

"Fine. Let's get to work," she said irritably.

Robby stood up and stretched his six foot frame to appear taller, pulling up on his pants. "Let's keep our heads about us, my dear. What do you say, Sandy? Aren't you interested in moving up here at Saxony?"

She frowned. And how was this relevant suddenly?

"Yes. But what does that have to do with anything?"

Robby looked annoyed. Still, he persisted. He danced around the large mahogany desk and pulled up another chair and scooted next to her.

"Just how well did you know Elizabeth Marx?" he asked pointedly.

Sandy wouldn't let him see her cave in. She held her own, taking a deep breath and hopping to her feet, standing very erect. She leaned against a window behind the desk, now clutching the legal pad to her chest.

"I've got the pen and paper," she said stiffly. "Let's go."

"You did know her, didn't you?"

"What does it matter now? The poor girl is dead."

"Well, that's insensitive," he said. "For someone who was friends with her."

"Look, Robby, you know everyone around here is uncomfortable about the tragedy. In fact, I don't know how anyone is able to work in this atmosphere. So why make it tougher."

Robby rounded the desk again. A flush of red anger had risen up his face to his neck.

"Tell me how well you knew Elizabeth, Sandy. They don't have any leads. Don't you want to know who murdered her?"

"You were the one who was here, Robby. You were one of the first people to reach the office."

"As were you. Elizabeth didn't know what was best for her anyway. I fostered her career. But she was unfocused. She had a lot of boyfriends. Did you know that? And some of them were pretty dangerous."

Sandy felt stifled, compressed like the wood in this large office. She started to feel smaller and smaller. She pushed off the window and raced for the door. But Robby jumped in front of her and took a firm hold of her wrists, his fingers tightening around them, pinching.

"You're going to tell me what you know," he said, his voice guttural. "I'm not going to walk around here, suspected by everyone. I'm sick of the stares. The woman was just like all the others. She wanted something from me and I gave it to her. I had no reason to kill her, for God's sake."

The door flew open all at once. Amanda stalked into the room.

"Excuse me," she said, eyeing Sandy who was pushed back. She massaged her wrists. "We have a few items from the meeting to talk about. They can't wait."

Robby glared at her. "It can wait, Amanda," he said.

Sandy slipped out of the office. She sat at her desk again, straightening papers, trying not to appear ruffled by the abusive encounter. Minutes later, she looked through the photographs. Something about the picture which she now knew to be Penelope Rutherford haunted her. She decided she needed to talk to Glenda about any information she might have. It seemed to teeter beyond curiosity now. The clothes, it was the clothes that got her. Why had Elizabeth Marx been dressed in those clothes? The aged blouse and the floor-length skirt. There had been something cynical or ironic about dressing the woman that way. Sandy recalled how hard Elizabeth worked, all the late hours with Robby and then her work at home for law school.

True, the gossip around the office had been that Elizabeth had been having an affair with him. But Sandy had still liked Elizabeth. She was always helpful with work and she had a way of laughing off stress. She also believed Robby had good reason to be leery of Sandy. Sandy had seen all the ugly arguments between the two and had heard them through his office door.

That office door swung open now. Amanda shut the door behind her. Then she stormed over to Sandy's desk. Leaning over, she tapped her pen on the desk.

"What's your problem, Sandy?" she asked.

Sandy looked up slowly. "What do you mean?"

"Robby is in enough trouble. He might be guilty of murder, for God's sake. So I don't know if he's ready for another affair with an assistant. Besides," she said sadistically, "look what happened to the last one. You don't want to anger him. Just behave and stick to business. You'll keep your job."

"You're either giving me really strong advice or you're threatening me."

"And for your own good," Amanda went on, "keep your mouth shut about what you know."

"You sound as if you're on your brother's side for once."

Amanda stopped. "What the hell is that supposed to mean?"

"It's practically public record that you don't get along with Robby."

"It seems you're getting along with Robby a little too well. You don't want to end up like Elizabeth Marx."

"What exactly do you know about the murder?"

"You, Sandy dear, were one of the people in early that day."

"And everyone knows," Sandy interrupted, "that Elizabeth was murdered around midnight."

"Approximately. The time frame actually covers about an hour. You could have been here." She stopped, her chest heaving. "I'm just telling you, women like you end up like Elizabeth."

Sandy frowned. Her phone rang. Amanda stalked off.

"Sandy. It's Jan. Brandy is standing outside my little house. She's there, right there in the yard and she's staring at the house."

"Calm down Jan. Are you sure she's not just walking her dog?"

"Do you think I'm crazy, Sandy?"

"No, of course not. I'm having my own little drama here at work."

Jan's voice dropped to a hoarse whisper. "What is happening there?"

"I think Robby is coming on to me sexually to try and throw me off the murder somehow."

"Yes, but you said he was always kind of after you, wasn't he? Even when Elizabeth was still alive?"

"Let's put it this way. Robby has always had a need to control the women in his personal life and at work." She lowered her voice when two executives passed by. "A couple of women were up for promotions recently. He somehow changed the course of all their careers. I know this from having talked to Elizabeth. Elizabeth knew a lot about the Saxony family. Probably too much. She knew how they conducted business as well as relationships. Sometimes I wonder if that was what got her killed."

Jan cleared her throat, her eyes still on Brandy as she stood resolutely at the edge of the lawn. "You really think it was someone within the company?"

"I don't know really. Supposedly Amanda has an alibi. She was with Sestina over at Brandy's house, which I find strange. Apparently, they're on friendly terms. It's odd to me. Amanda doesn't appear to have many friends but somehow she knew Sestina from another couple out in New York. She introduced her to Robby and Brandy."

"And then what about Robby? Is it just my having seen him? Is that why he's harassing me?"

Sandy lowered her voice and grasped the mouthpiece with both hands. "His supposed alibi is some crony here who claims he and Robby were working late on a project. Your having seen him in the garage first at twelve and then not again until one or so really could kill his alibi. He'd already made up an alibi not knowing that you'd seen him. Now he could get caught in a lie."

"Do you think that's why Brandy is watching me? To scare me into sticking to what I saw? I mean I don't even know if she's on Robby's side or my side."

"I doubt that's why. I think she has her own agenda."

Jan walked to the window again and peeked around the curtains. She could see the tousled bleached hair and the fur jacket.

"The woman hasn't changed her clothes for days. I'm convinced of that. What is going on with her?"

"What time are you going to the movies?"

"At seven. Sure you don't want to come?"

"No, thanks. But I'm tempted. I'd like to look over these pictures some more. I have to go. The light on the intercom is on. I'm being paged by the god Robby himself."

"I don't know how you work for him."

"Well, now, I have my reasons. You'll see."

Sandy stood up, smoothing her skirt. She clenched her fists and walked to the door. Entering, she found Robby seated on the sofa next to his desk.

"Brandy just confessed to me that she had your friend Jan Gates and someone called Glenda Morgan go to River Falls and appraise some Saxony antiques. Is that true? And if it is, what the hell business is it of yours?"

"I don't know what you mean."

"What exactly are you trying to find out about the Saxony family?"

CHAPTER EIGHT

"I don't know," Jan said. "The whole ordeal with Robby really unnerves me. I just don't want Robby to think he's got the better of me."

Jan rubbed her arms in the cool dusk. She, Glenda, and Sandy waited outside the Round Theater in Rosedale for a double feature Monty Python night.

"I'm glad you decided to come with us," she told Sandy. "So you think Robby is coming on to you now because he wants to hide something? And he thinks he can warm you up to him?"

"Well, he's always flirted with me," Sandy confessed. "But now there's an urgency about it. But what's really creepy, and he knows it, is that his alibi of working on a project all night with a co-worker the night of the murder doesn't mesh with when you say you saw him in his garage. He opened his mouth too soon. He's certainly placed doubt in the minds of the police. What do you think, Glenda?"

Glenda nodded, looking thoughtful. As the line moved slowly, she looked around. The usual types of Python fans, quirky intellectuals, milled about wearing jeans, university t-shirts, and sneakers. Round Theater was located on Drake Drive, a congested street, and she watched first a Ford Taurus and then a BMW pass by, reflecting the many facets of Rosedale.

"I think Robby is definitely getting sloppy," Jan continued. "From what you've told me, Sandy, he's always been a smooth player. But now he seems upended somehow. It's like he doesn't know what his next move should be. And I think that concept is new to him."

Sandy agreed, crossing her arms over her chest. Her intense blue eyes looked past Glenda as if she were deep in thought. Glenda noticed the woman's arched eyebrows and strong cheekbones. She reminded her of some vamp out of film noir.

Jan said very little. In fact, Glenda noticed her friend was quite jittery and was perpetually playing with her hair, particularly fixing and refixing locks behind her ears.

Glenda turned to her. "Are you all right?"

Jan's hands shook as she ran her fingers through her short blonde bangs. Her nose was sunburned from working in her garden.

"I'm fine."

"You aren't yourself. Are you taking cold medication?"

"What do you mean?" she snapped.

"You just seem, well, preoccupied."

Jan nodded absently, staring beyond Glenda across the street. "I had a glass of wine before I left the house. So what? It's to take the edge off."

How many times had Glenda heard that before in her life? Certainly an old excuse from many a drinker. Glenda knew from her own alcoholism and subsequent recovery. She followed Jan's gaze across the street. Suddenly, Jan grabbed Glenda's arm.

"I knew it. There she is."

She pointed behind them in line to someone further back. Glenda looked. Sandy stood on her toes. "Where, Jan?" she asked trying to placate.

Jan's voice grew hysterical. "Why is she doing this to me? It's Brandy. And this time she's got a goon with her. Some big guy."

Glenda spotted them immediately when she noticed a brutish-looking man towering above the rest of the line. He had bleached blond hair like Brandy's.

"You think Brandy is here looking for you?" Glenda asked.

But Jan had her hand to her mouth. Then her eyes widened. "Here they come," she whispered.

"Hello, neighbor," Brandy said. "Aren't you going to introduce me to your friends?"

Jan took a deep breath. "This is Sandy Larson. She works for your husband now. And this is Glenda Morgan."

"You're Glenda!" Brandy said, extending a jewel-covered hand. "It's nice to finally meet you. I just checked my storage facility yesterday. Quite a load of stuff the Saxony family hangs on to, isn't it? Thank you for helping me out with some of the antiques."

"And who is your friend?" Glenda said.

"This man? He's Rocko. Rocko is a friend of the family. A very close friend."

"You like Python, Rocko?" Glenda asked pointedly.

The three women were still chuckling as they walked into the theater minutes later.

"You had Rocko figured out," Sandy said.

"Don't think he's a true Python fan," Glenda said. "In fact, I'm starting to agree with you, Jan."

"That she's following me?" she asked.

Glenda nodded, her eyes following the petite blonde being trailed by her much larger companion. Rocko looked around, continually eying those in the row behind him, watching Glenda and her two companions from where they sat several rows behind them. They waited for Brandy to sit first. Once themselves seated, however, Brandy and Rocko stood up and moved behind them. "There's no doubt you're right, Jan."

Jan nodded. Her hands trembled in her lap. "What is it all about?"

"It's because," Sandy said, her voice low, "you can put holes in Robby's alibi."

Jan started breathing heavily.

"Jan," Glenda said, "would you like to get out of here?"

"I'm sorry. Can we wait until the movie starts and sneak out?"

The two nodded. Twenty minutes of previews and dancing hot dogs passed across the screen. Finally, the three women snuck out, one by one, as if going to the bathroom. Meeting outside, they ran the first two blocks.

"I feel like high school kids sneaking out of the house," Glenda said. "I think we can slow down now."

Late fall in Rosedale always promised a stray scent of burning leaves or a fireplace. The three walked along briskly, Glenda's clogs making dragging sounds on the sidewalk. Several times Jan checked behind them.

"My car is a block away," Glenda said. "There's a coffee house nearby. Want to stop there?"

"I don't know," Jan said. "Maybe I should just go home."

Sandy kicked at the leaves and shook her head. "Then you're giving in to their strong-arm tactic."

"Do you think Robby knows Brandy has been following me?" Jan asked, surprised.

79

"No, I don't think so," Glenda said.

Sandy looked at her. "Why not?"

"Because Brandy was very secretive about the Saxony antiques she had me appraise. I'm certain she didn't want Robby to know about my bringing them back. She pretended like it was a surprise for him but I doubt it. I don't think he knew anything about it at first. She just mentioned a small appraisal."

Half an hour later the three sat over steaming mugs of coffee at the Rosedale Diner. Sandy pulled out the photographs Glenda had copied for her.

"There's something about these. Did you notice this one?" Sandy asked, handing it to Glenda.

Glenda recognized the double shot for the stereoscope with the telling photograph of Penelope Rutherford on the right-hand side.

"Yes, I definitely recognize that. That's the odd picture of the woman who supposedly was suspected of being the real killer of William Saxony. She went unnoticed by the press. Eliza Mortimer was much more colorful as the accused and her family had comparatively little money or clout. Eliza was hanged for the murder of William."

"So that's why this Penelope was overlooked?"

"From what I understood from the older woman in River Falls, you know, the Dodie Carmichael character, Penelope came from the right kind of folks. Her family background allowed everything to be very hush-hush. And from what I understand, Eliza Mortimer was moving up at the company. She started as a typewriter, what they called typists in those days. Then a relationship developed with William, but Eliza wasn't terribly interested in him. Dodie Carmichael made it clear to me that Penelope Rutherford was also involved with him, but that she did not take to being dumped as easily as Eliza. She worked in the factory trying to mingle among the other factory level girls. She wanted to fit in but soon it was clear she suffered from a severe mental disorder. Penelope was what you'd call now a borderline personality. Psychologically speaking, she wanted to divide and conquer. She was obsessed with William."

"Do you think Brandy wanted to find out something about the family history?" Jan inquired meekly.

"I wonder if she was looking for something to do with an inheritance?" Sandy said.

"I know her first priority was to assess the monetary value of the antiques. That makes me wonder if the Saxonys are in some sort of money trouble," Glenda commented. "Let me see those pictures again. The copies I made for you."

"Sure."

Sandy handed over the photographs. "There was something I noticed, or thought I did."

Glenda flipped through them, pausing to smile at a few group shots of benevolent-looking faces of young men and women. Then she stopped.

"This one," she said.

She handed it around to Sandy who looked at it and said, "It's interesting. It looks like Eliza Mortimer. It's that same round face and curly brown hair. And she wears glasses, too. But how can this be?"

Jan was afraid to look. "What is it?"

"Glenda," Sandy said, "you know what I mean, don't you?"

Glenda nodded. "She's wearing a dress from the 1920s. The decor in the room and the car in front of the house where she's sitting—it looks like years later."

"But it's Eliza Mortimer. She's the slasher, isn't she?"

"Well, that's the woman they claim was the slasher. But we know differently now. It wasn't this Eliza woman."

"But she was accused of killing several men in the factory. They were like rituals," Jan said.

Glenda started. "Why did you use that word? Was that specifically what Eliza was accused of?"

Jan looked fearful. "Well, that's what old Joseph told me at the cottage. He said that it was a ritual Eliza was known for. But they were just folk tales, not facts."

"What kind of rituals though?" Glenda paused, her excitement overwhelming Jan. "The reason I ask is because, of all people, Dodie Carmichael mentioned something, and made a connection between a ritual and the way in which Elizabeth Marx was found."

Jan's eyes widened. She reached for her coffee, her hands shaking. Although the atmosphere of the diner was one of benign sounds of clinking silverware and water glasses, the look in Jan's eyes was something like primal fear.

"How would this Dodie Carmichael have known about the recent

81

murder at Saxony?" Sandy asked.

Glenda merely studied the photo of Eliza Mortimer, interpreting the eyes as intelligent but replete with rage.

"And what kind of ritual," Glenda wondered aloud, "would have been perpetuated by the death of Elizabeth Marx? And why does this simple photo of Eliza Mortimer bother me so much?"

She rubbed her forehead, deep in thought. "There is a connection between River Falls and the cabin there, and the relationship between William Saxony and Eliza Mortimer. But why did Brandy want me to go through those things in the cabin? Why was it so urgent?"

Sandy nodded. "It's as if she wanted to bring you into the Saxony story somehow."

"Do you think the appraisal of the antiques was a pretense?" Glenda asked.

"Maybe," Sandy murmured. "Her only other motive, I guess, would have been the money from the items. But I don't think she and Robby are hurting for money."

The waitress poured more coffee, giving an extra glance at the suddenly silent women, all three sitting quietly. Jan's movements were jerky now. Her face was pale.

"Not only is Dodie familiar with what's happened at the former Saxony factory but so, apparently, is old Joseph," Glenda said.

"As if there's a spy or something, you mean?" Sandy asked.

"It may be simply someone who keeps Dodie and Joseph up to the minute with information about the Saxonys. For instance," Glenda said, "how did Brandy know there were antiques up at the cottage anyway? How did she know about the cottage? Jan, you've known the Saxonys for many years, isn't that right?"

"Yes," she said, nodding, her eyes pensive.

"What about Amanda Saxony? Sandy?"

"Let me tell you about her," Sandy said. "She's a vampire. I mean it's true that Saxony is archaic when it comes to promoting women, but she doesn't know how to get ahead as a woman or make use of her qualities. She thinks she has to be a vulture, a misconception it seems of many a businesswoman in my opinion. Some people have said she's possessed when it comes to her job. She's been known to spend the night at the office. She'll call colleagues in the company repeatedly without waiting for return calls. She walks in on people in the middle of meetings. And then when she meets the clients, she's the polite professional to their faces, even though she's stabbed most of them in the back behind closed doors."

"Do you think she's been involved in unseemly business practices?"

"Absolutely," Sandy said. "There were many nights she'd meet in her locked office with unknown persons until late into the evening. She never knew I was still there past eleven at night."

The three women pondered these words in silence. Jan looked up, her face draining of color. Glenda followed her gaze. Brandy and her menacing escort walked outside the diner. All three women ducked under the table.

"Well," Glenda said, "aren't we brave. Guess what girls, it's time for a little breaking and entering."

"What?" Jan said meekly, still under the table.

Sandy sat up again. "What's your devious plan?" she asked.

Glenda was serious. "It's time we took a closer look at the Saxony offices that were once a deadly factory."

Half an hour later, the three young women stood with their backs to the front door of Saxony Clothiers. Located in the warehouse district of town, there were not many cars to be seen. They waited, however, for one small Chevy Cavalier that had decided to take a backroads route.

"Now, let's go," Glenda said, hopping to the door. It had two locks on it. She worked the first one with a credit card. "I don't know, this second lock is beyond my expertise. Is there any other way in?"

"There's a side door," Sandy said. "Sometimes the lock doesn't catch when it closes. People sneak in and out of it all day to smoke cigarettes outside."

"Let's look."

Reaching the side of the building, Glenda pulled on the side door. "Unfortunately, you have a responsible smoker at Saxony who closed the door after a quick puff."

Glenda looked around. "With the fall weather, there's a chance someone may have cracked a window somewhere. There's no air conditioning and certainly no heat on yet."

"Over here," she said excitedly. "Do you know where that window goes Sandy?"

"It's the men's bathroom, I think. Yes. That's it. The women's bathroom is on the other side."

"Let's go," Glenda said.

"Go where?" Jan said hesitantly. "It's the second floor!"

Glenda was already pulling over barrels and large bins toward the window. Sandy helped her. Soon Glenda was climbing up, and within fifteen minutes, the three women stood inside the factory.

They rushed through the place. "Here's my desk," Sandy said.

"What are we looking for?" Jan asked.

"I'm most interested," Glenda whispered, "in Mr. Robby Saxony's office, and Amanda's office too. Either office or both of them could yield something of interest. I'm going to start with Amanda's. Where's her office, Sandy?"

"Down the hall," she said, pointing. "That way. But we have to be quiet. I know they have a security service. A couple of men in cars drive by the factory section now and then. So keep the lights low. They know people work at odd hours so they keep an eye out."

Glenda nodded. But she was only half listening. She had entered Amanda's office and suddenly had a strange, uncomfortable feeling about the place. She pulled her jacket tightly around her, feeling cold all at once. Perhaps because she had open-minded family living in California, she believed certain places had bad auras or karma. Now she believed this room had something evil lurking in its past that permeated the place. The sudden cold. It made her wonder about the precise location of the women who had died in the tragic fire years before. What stresses possessed these walls?

Glenda pressed on, walking swiftly behind a large black onyx desk and chair set. Then she stopped. It was there on a back wall, hardly noticeable unless one looked for it. It was a photograph of Eliza Mortimer standing firmly in a steadfast position, hand on her hip and wearing a dress of layers of lace and the signature glasses. It occurred to Glenda that Amanda featured Eliza in several pictures, three along the back wall. As she continued to peruse the room, a growing nausea overtook her, that same strange feeling she'd had before.

And the more she stared at the photograph of Eliza, the more it seemed to move. The pale white pictured face changed expression somehow, the lacy dress moving. Glenda turned away. She was obviously overwrought.

Along the far wall opposite the desk were several group photos of women dressed in a similar fashion. Beneath the photos the captions read "1896 employees—Saxony Skirt Company" and "Company Picnic 1903." In the latter photo Glenda could easily pick out Eliza Mortimer. As the pictures continued on to the right however, they grew more strange.

Then the thought hit her. Glenda wondered at the appropriateness of such photos being in an office environment. She continued to walk back to a corner hidden behind a jutting-out section of the wall. There were three or four photographs hidden away in a far corner. One photo depicted Eliza Mortimer under arrest, handcuffed and being led away into custody. There was also a newspaper clipping about the trial and eventual conviction of Eliza.

Amanda's interest in the case bordered clearly on obsession. Glenda walked swiftly to another wall and there were smaller photographs of William Saxony, the founder, and then Amanda's father Richard Saxony, and Robby's early days in the company.

Pretty routine office otherwise, she figured. Except that gnawing sensation about the place that something was not right. All at once, she realized how dead quiet the place was. She slipped back into the hallway. Much too quiet.

"Sandy? Where are you both?"

"What the hell are you doing?" said a low voice.

CHAPTER NINE

"Who's there?"

Glenda had seen it briefly—the silhouette of someone. But now she looked and there was no one.

"Hello?"

Footsteps sounded down the hall. She stepped back, clinging to the wall.

"Glenda? Are you still in Amanda's office?" Sandy said in a hoarse whisper. "I can't find Jan."

"Did you just say something to me?"

"When?"

"Just now. Did you ask me what I was doing?"

"Glenda? What are you talking about?"

"Nothing. I must be nervous. Let's get back to work. What have you found?"

"I covered Robby's office. I know all the workings of his inner sanctum let's just say."

Glenda nodded and returned to Amanda's office. Bending over she checked all the file cabinets. They were locked. Sliding open the long middle drawer of the desk, she felt around for keys, then tracing her palm along the top of the drawer she found a key taped there. Figuring it fit one of the drawers of the desk, she soon successfully unlocked a deep drawer located to the left of the center drawer containing files.

She leafed through them quickly. Most of them read "Corporate Head Meeting," "Executive Meetings," "Monthly Operating Reports." All pretty routine. Until she found one shoved under the hanging folders. It was a red file with frayed edges. It read "Eliza Mortimer b. 1883—?"

Date of death?

Glenda was struck. She held the file in her hand, bewildered.

Why wouldn't there be a date of death? She opened the file and leaned over a desk light, bending it down so as not to shine throughout the room. She found more photos of Eliza Mortimer, the usual one of her posing in the cavalier stance, her hand on one hip. But there were many more; humorous photos of her seated at her typewriter and pictures of her talking to a lanky man with a thin long mustache. Glenda knew him to be William Saxony. Then behind the photos were several newspaper clippings detailing the tortuous trial of "Eliza the Slasher," as they called her. Apparently Eliza's name was coined because several female co-workers had claimed they'd seen her shaving Mr. Saxony with a cut-throat—the razor blade of the day.

Then Glenda found another file, located behind the Eliza file. It was labeled with a question mark. Inside Glenda found another photo of Eliza Mortimer except this one was labeled 1923. She wore the same type of lacy drop-waist dress with a pleated skirt. Even the frames of the glasses were the same—Oxford tortoise.

Apparently this woman, who also referred to herself as Eliza Mortimer, had secured a job at Saxony. Then life grew strange in the hitherto safe confines of Northwoods. A series of "slasher" murders had gripped the town. Articles sprang up surrounding the original Eliza. Several old-timers at Saxony claimed they recognized her. One article even asked, "Has she come back?" and another claimed, "One death didn't do the job."

This was insane. Did the mainstream society of Rosedale and Northwoods really believe Eliza hadn't died or that she'd come back somehow? How could so many persons have believed these fantastic stories?

Glenda noticed that her hand trembled where she clutched the file. Then footsteps sounded in the room. She dropped it to the hardwood floor.

"Who's there?"

"Glenda," Sandy said, "I found something very bizarre. You have to see this."

Sandy raced over to her. "I've found divorce papers. It looks like Robby has filed for divorce from our dear Brandy."

"What about Brandy?" Jan said from behind them.

"That's what I wonder now too," Glenda said, not missing the tremulous tone of Jan's voice. "Are you thinking, Jan, that Brandy is trailing you out of some sort of suspicion?"

"Yes. Maybe she thinks I'm involved with Robby somehow."

"From what I've heard," Glenda said, "it could be any number of women who are involved with Robby. Brandy must be aware of all his dalliances, surely?"

The three women sat in Amanda's office, in what should have been silence. And yet there came a humming sound.

"What kind of machine is that?" Jan asked.

Sandy shook her head. "I've never noticed it during the day at work. It's always so busy around here."

Glenda hesitated. Then she stood up and walked around the office which was adorned with abrasive abstract paintings and the token black and white photographs of the ancestors. "You're both going to think I'm strange but there is something about this office that strikes me as peculiar."

"I've never been allowed in here," Sandy said, her voice hushed. "She keeps the door locked even if she's just going down the hall to a meeting. And she never holds meetings in her office. She always gets a conference room."

"Interesting," Glenda said. "Because have you noticed the pictures she has hanging in here?"

Sandy and Jan approached the walls slowly. Sandy nodded as she walked along. "A few about the history of the company," she said, "and a particular interest in Eliza Mortimer."

"But why exactly?"

"Come here," Glenda said, walking to the right side of the office. She put her palm on the wall. "It feels wet here. There's something here."

"What?" Jan said, sounding alarmed.

"My God," Glenda said, looking at her palm. "There's some sort of red stain on my hand."

Glenda raced to the desk and picked up a box of Kleenex. She wiped her hand. "I think it's paint. But why would someone have painted over these bricks?"

"They're trying to hide something," Sandy suggested. "And you know what? Follow me."

The three women stepped out into the hallway and turned left. Darkness enveloped them as they walked farther and farther down the hallway.

"What is this?" Jan asked.

"It's a door," Sandy said. "Come here, Glenda. Try it. It's always locked. I've never seen anyone from the company go in here. In fact, most of the administrative assistants won't even walk down this hallway. One feels kind of eerie in this hallway."

Glenda tried the door. It was locked solidly. Then she felt around the sides. "For that matter," she said to Sandy, "it's been sealed. Look at this, some sort of rubber or similar substance has been filled in to the gaps around the doorframe. Someone has sealed this door shut."

"Which means no one has ever gone in there?" Jan said, her voice wavering.

"Not for years, probably," Glenda affirmed.

"But why would a room like this be located here on company property?"

"Remember," Glenda said, "this was originally the factory. This was the same factory where a crime took place—the crime of ten women dying in a terrible fire because of poor working conditions."

The three women stood there. Again, all three were thoughtful. Jan had backed up a bit, and stood in the partial light of a green banker's desk lamp. Sandy leaned against the wall with her arms crossed over her chest and watched Glenda. Glenda felt around the door, her fingers groping around the seal, then sniffed the area. "It's old. It's an older type of rubber I think. It's deteriorating in certain spots like here and here," she said, pointing. "Someone definitely wants it kept closed, forever."

"Let's go into the hallway again."

Glenda led the way back up the hall toward the office again. It was the same corridor which led to the locked door. "You see how this is side by side with Amanda's office?"

"What are you saying?" Sandy asked sarcastically. "Something is bleeding into the wall?"

"No, of course not. I think someone has painted the bricks recently in Amanda's office to cover up trying to get into the locked room without anyone knowing. Amanda for instance. Maybe someone tried from inside her office—to see what was behind the brick."

"Maybe it was Brandy. That would explain why she was so insistent about our going up to River Falls. Maybe she's stashing family heirlooms for her own gain.

"I never noticed these group photos, Sandy," Jan said. "All those times I met you for lunch. Why didn't we see it?"

"Why?" Sandy said, leaning over to see what Jan was looking at. "What do you see?"

"It's a photograph of new employees from 2001," Jan said. "And here's one from another office. I didn't know they had a River Falls location."

"Do they?" Glenda asked, walking over. "And, my God," she said, "look at this photograph."

The three women peered in the semi-darkness, the only light coming from the alley outside. At the end of the first line of women, there was one in the photo whose face, height, and build were identical to "Eliza the Slasher."

"It can't be," Jan muttered. Her voice was tremulous. She moved to the door and was already pushing it open.

"It can't be," Sandy repeated. "Wait, Jan. Calm yourself."

Glenda leaned over again, squinting directly at the photograph. She had to lean left and right because of the glass glare. "I'm certain the woman in the photo is identical to Eliza Mortimer. So we had her in 1903, then she was apparently hanged for murder and came back again in 1923, and now in 2001. It's eerie, I'll admit."

*****

Out on the street again, the three women walked along swiftly, passing under low hanging branches of elm trees, the remaining greenery moist and the sound of leaves crunching under their feet. Soon they spotted Glenda's old Volvo located two streets over. All three piled in.

"Shall I drop you off first, Jan?" Glenda asked.

"That's fine." She paused, then said, "May I ask you something? What do you think about the idea of Eliza Mortimer coming back in the 1920s? Is it crazy? Was it mass hysteria? I mean, what happened to that woman, anyway?"

Glenda nodded, and simultaneously checked Sandy's expression seated next to her. "The woman caused enough of a stir in 1920s

Northwoods for her to be arrested and questioned. I read this in an article I found in Amanda's office. But they couldn't hold her on anything."

"Do you think it was her? You know, the slasher? Eliza Mortimer?"

Then Jan's voice changed. "Maybe she came back because of unfinished business."

"Who knows."

"You know what I think?" Glenda said. "I think the people in 1923 believed it to be Eliza Mortimer. I think Amanda Saxony believes it was Eliza and is fearful even now that she will come back."

"Amanda Saxony? Why would she believe such nonsense?" Sandy insisted.

"Because she's susceptible to spirits and the netherworld. She'll try anything that will give her power," Glenda said.

"We need to get access to that locked room. There must be a way. And what happened to the clothes Elizabeth Marx was wearing when they found her body in the office? You know, the long skirt and the blouse?"

"All the evidence is with the police," Sandy said. "I can only tell you what I heard, the gossip. Elizabeth Marx had her eye on moving up. Not to just any job. Eventually she wanted to be a co-partner at the top. I suppose Robby could have had a motive to keep her out of the picture, couldn't he?"

"Especially if he sensed she had the brain power and the education to keep moving up. Didn't you tell me that the company has been losing money since Robby has been in charge? Someone new coming in with novel ideas and a fresh law degree could ruin him."

"Yes. On top of that, his father turned the company over to him in 1995. It was served up on the proverbial silver platter. Revenues have been bad ever since, to say the least. The executive conference room is glass. Lately, we assistants have been privy to the meetings and how they progress, or not. I have witnessed many a disagreement. And lately, it's about something Robby has screwed up."

The three women piled into the car. Jan chewed her thumb nail nervously and slumped in the passenger seat next to Glenda. The night felt cool and sunless. The air was a frosty visible exhale. Jan looked mournfully into the right rearview mirror. Then she leaned forward, her eyes wide.

"It's her for God's sake!"

"Who? Where?"

"In the black Lexus behind us. Don't turn around," she said, when Glenda also looked in the rearview mirror.

"Brandy you mean?" Glenda asked, her voice low.

"I know her car."

"Should I drop you at home or shall I keep going to throw her off?"

"I can't run from her all the time. Just take me home," Jan said, near tears.

Soon they pulled up to the coach house. The main house in front was an English Tudor. The owner, a fifty-ish woman, stood out front of the property.

"Do you know your landlord well enough to go for a visit?" Glenda asked.

"I know her a little. Let me out here and I'll go right over and see her."

Jan jumped from the car and gave Glenda a quick wave. Glenda watched the petite woman walk inside the landlord's white kitchen. The scene gave off a feeling of security and permanence like a bright glow emanating from the dark backdrop of sunset. It was good to see her friend in a spacious and refined kitchen, in a house so superior in its antiquity to the ludicrous excess of the Saxony house across the street.

As they drove off, Glenda slowed when she noticed Brandy's black Lexus already back in the driveway. In the back yard, made visible by bright flood lights, Brandy walked a small circle under small, newly planted trees. Her arms flailed as she talked on a fuchsia cellular phone. She wore leather pants and a leather jacket. As she walked on a small patch of land, her black square-toed boots dug into the ground. Glenda didn't see the small giant she'd had escorting her around all day.

"What's her deal?" Glenda said to Sandy.

Sandy shook her head.

"I was wondering," she said, then hesitated, "if you'd heard anything about rituals associated with the Saxony family."

Glenda's eyes widened. "I thought it was strange. It's something that the Dodie Carmichael woman said. You know, the woman that lives in the converted church in River Falls? She claimed the murder of Elizabeth Marx was some ritual act. It really stunned me when she said it. And how would she know, anyway?"

Sandy nodded, looking thoughtful.

"Why do you ask?"

"Because of what I read in the newspapers about Elizabeth's condition when they found her. And supposedly the last person she saw that day was Robby Saxony. After her birthday celebration across the street, he called her back to the office No one else saw her after that. So she must have showed up at the office again in the middle of the night. Did she come back for some reason? The cops said someone undressed her and changed her clothes after she was dead."

"How morbid."

"It was like a sacrifice or something. The old clothes themselves are some sort of message," Glenda went on.

The two women were sitting now out front of Sandy's condo.

"Why would anyone go to all the trouble to dress someone up? And especially like that? It was as if someone was mocking Elizabeth or making a statement about her character in some way. What do you think?" Sandy said.

"That much is clear. But what was she doing back at the office in the middle of the night? Did she live alone?"

"She did," Sandy said. "And the place was comfortably furnished by Mr. Robby Saxony himself. Whatever she wanted— antiques, mission style, French Provincial. I guess he helped out quite a bit with the mortgage too. I ran across the invoices in her desk once," she said, grinning.

"And she was in law school, right? She sounds too independent to take anything, monetary or otherwise, from a man."

"Let's put it this way, she wore pink sweaters and pearls and little pink shoes by day. Robby seemed happy with that. But she was in law school at night. She was moving up. He was threatened, certainly. Especially since she'd become very tight with several of the executives. All the people throwing her the birthday party had introduced her to some key folks in the legal department. They'd consulted her on her business savvy."

"You say she was intelligent, but she liked to be taken care of?" Glenda asked.

"True, to a point. She wanted her independence and the security.

I know she sounds like a contradiction. Amanda had a real problem with her."

Glenda was interested. She eyed Sandy slowly. "Why would Elizabeth matter to Amanda if she was only an assistant?"

"Because she was an assistant to Robby and Robby represents a major hurdle to Amanda in reaching her goal of taking over the company."

"Interesting."

"I have to go," Sandy said. "We'll talk soon."

The women parted. The next morning, Sandy showed up early to work. The clock on her desk said 7:00 A.M. Even so, a light from Robby's office could be seen under his closed door. She recalled ruefully that he had a big presentation early in the morning. She had to be prepared to be overworked at any moment. Soon his wooden door opened and he stalked out.

"I need forty copies of this, stapled and," he said and ran his hand through his hair. He looked preoccupied. "Bring them into the meeting in the executive board room by 7:30, got that?"

"Of course."

He didn't make eye contact; in fact, he never turned his head. Instead he stared at the conference room, making note of who had already arrived. Within seconds, he'd rushed off. All that lingered was the pungent scent of too much after-shave and lotion.

Sandy stood up and prepared to make the copies.

CHAPTER TEN

It was now nearing 7:30 P.M. Sandy continued to clear away paperclips from her desk and rearrange the stapler and post-it notes—again and again. She could still see the executives in the glass conference room milling about, making suggestions, forcing polite opinions. They were fish in an aquarium. The meeting had been "finishing up" for the past three hours.

Then she opened the drawer and pulled out the small envelope of photos again. Flipping through them, she noticed a group shot. Someone in the photo struck her as unusual. She picked up the phone to call Glenda.

"Hi, Sandy," Glenda said. "Why are you still at the office?"

"How did you know it was me? Caller I.D., of course. Look. Do you have the photos you copied for me lying around somewhere nearby?"

"Let me get them," Glenda said, rising from her overstuffed reading chair. She retrieved the photos from her messy rolltop desk. "Here they are. Shoot."

"Well, there's a group photograph in the back and I'd swear the woman looks familiar but, more importantly, tell me what you think of the clothes."

"Hold on, let me find it." Glenda flipped through the last set of pictures and finally came to the group shots near the end. "It says here 'Keystone View Company, Copyright Publisher.' Then it lists a bunch of cities. One of them is River Falls, Illinois. And here are the group shots. Which one?"

"It's a picture of a group with an elderly woman standing in the back. This didn't make sense to me. But if you study the picture very closely, it's not an older woman at all, Sandy. It's a young woman of about twenty and she has white hair."

"Yes. And do you recognize the face? Maybe you haven't seen

her before, but that's Penelope Rutherford. Remember the story
Dodie Carmichael gave me about an attempted exorcism performed
on Penelope in the church basement? This is the same church which
Dodie now calls her home."

"But notice, too," Sandy said. "The clothes."

Glenda looked, holding the photo under the stained glass prairie
lamp on her side table. "It appears to be your typical Victorian flair
skirt to the floor and a high collar, little lacy blouse, and a cameo."

"Listen to this, Glenda. I was here first thing that morning,
remember? The morning they found Elizabeth Marx. She was
wearing an identical blouse with the same light pattern and that same
chain with something tucked in her pocket."

"What that is," Glenda said, "is a watch and chain with a fob
attached to it. They were decorative and often expensive talismans or
charms that were worn at the bottom of chains attached to a pocket
watch. What's interesting though is that they were worn strictly by
men. But notice her white hair? The only way I've heard of prema-
ture grey or white is from a shock to one's system—some severe
trauma. She didn't have white hair in the earlier pictures. It's just in
this group shot that it shows up."

"And what about the fob? Why is she wearing that?"

"Well, it could be to make herself more masculine, or maybe
she's wearing it because it belonged to a man. Could be even a man
all the women knew. I do know though, after examining Amanda
Saxony's office, that she is quite interested in the history of the
Saxony family and money. Not only were there pictures of Eliza
Mortimer and articles describing the case against her, but some group
photos in the drawer, hidden at the very bottom with some of
Penelope Rutherford. What is it about these women that seems to
fascinate both Amanda and Robby?"

"You're right about that," Sandy whispered. "Robby is a real head
case. He brags about the men in the family and implies that all the
women were hanging by threads, quite insane, you know?"

Glenda perused the pictures some more. There was silence at the
other end of the phone. Sandy gazed at the door as it swung open and
the group of co-workers filed out.

"I have to go," Sandy said quickly, then added softly, "I have my
own agenda for tonight."

"What are you up to?" Glenda asked.

But Sandy had already hung up the phone.

"Did everything go well?" she asked Robby as he whisked past to return to his office.

"Come in my office now," he ordered.

Sandy settled into a leather chair demurely. She sat opposite his desk.

"Let me ask you something," he said. "It's off the record too. It's between us. Do you understand?"

"Yes."

"How well did you know Elizabeth Marx?"

"Very well. Of course I didn't know her as well as you did."

He nodded impatiently. "There's something odd going on around here. I've been getting strange phone calls from someone named P. Rutherford. Look at these messages," he said, throwing ten or so slips of paper up in the air. "And someone named Eileen Reynolds. As far as the first name is concerned I have no clue who that is. The second name though, sounds familiar. I think she's at another location at Saxony Clothiers. I want you to find her. Find out about her and get me a picture of her."

"Why don't you just return her calls, Robby?" Sandy said, somewhat annoyed.

Robby stood up straight, adjusting his suspenders. He strutted about the office, looking out the windows. He was well-built and trim, and his suits were cut of the finest silk. All the Saxony executives dressed in the sharpest suits Saxony Clothiers had to offer. In spite of her growing disgust with Robby, it was hard not to notice his extreme good looks: the sharp nose and square chin and brooding but steely blue eyes. She'd overlook this attraction now.

"Just get me the information about this Eileen Reynolds and let it go at that."

He was literally scared. She'd never known him to be afraid of anything.

"She's really harassing you, is she?" Sandy asked.

"The woman keeps calling. How much do you know about Amanda, anyway?"

Sandy grimaced. "Wouldn't you know your own sister better than I would?"

"Don't give me a hard time. I know you were close to Elizabeth. And I know you're in on the happenings around this place. What have you heard?"

"I can't tell you that."

He slammed his hand on the desk. Sandy jumped.

"Damn it! Don't play games with me. You're just an administrator. You don't know how important this is. Who the hell do you think you are?"

Sandy bristled instantly. His demeanor changed. He stepped around the mammoth desk smoothly. The size of the desk was enormous, ridiculously so. It was a gargantuan desk for a gargantuan ego.

"Come on, my dear," he said, sitting casually on the corner of the desk.

Now was her chance.

"You don't know me very well," Sandy said, walking toward him, "do you? We can fix that."

He slipped off the corner of the desk and nearly hit the floor. He caught his balance swiftly, deftly, like some competitive skater.

"What did you say?"

She swallowed slowly. "Yes. Let's get dinner at Antonio's. It's late and you've had a rough meeting."

This fire could be dangerous.

His eyes pierced through her, exuding not desire but fear.

"Too out in the open, my dear. Let's go to a little hideaway I know about."

"Let's start with dinner, Robby. Don't get ahead of yourself."

But Robby had already walked to the door and grabbed his suit jacket from a hook on the back. Although the office had approved casual business dress on Fridays, the Saxony executives refused to adopt the relaxed look and instead wore the prime cut suits, the best designers had to offer. Robby Saxony in particular felt that style was his forte. In essence, that was where Robby looked for quality; whatever was on the outside was the most important. Which was why these strange women calling him was so unnerving. Perhaps they'd seen a picture of him in the quarterly report and had just lost their heads.

"You surprise me," Sandy said bravely.

Robby straightened his jacket, grabbed his wallet from the desk drawer, and opened the door. "Get your stuff," he said brusquely.

Sandy slipped out to her desk. She could see the light in Amanda's office was still on.

They drove together in Robby's black Jaguar. Soon they were seated at Antonio's. Just after the food arrived, Robby pulled out his cellular phone.

"Hi, Brandy," he said. "I'm going to be late again."

"Well, you got another call from a woman," she said bitterly.

"What? Who was it?"

"Someone named Eileen."

His face changed. Sandy tapped her steak with her fork. She tried to look disinterested. So much with the mystery surrounding Elizabeth's murder was impenetrable. Too many puzzles not making sense. But there was something about Saxony and those running it that made her fear for her life. She too could end up like Elizabeth.

"Did she leave a number?" he asked irritably.

"I'm sure you've got it!" she said, hanging up the phone.

He slammed his cellular shut and shoved it back in his breast pocket. Throwing his fork down on his plate, he downed his wine in one gulp and poured more from the bottle into his glass.

Sandy wished for some of Glenda's wisdom at this moment. Ever since Jan had introduced her, she'd come to respect Glenda's intuition. Something about Glenda's daring had impressed her. She had to think quickly now.

"I can find out who this woman is who keeps bothering you."

"What woman?"

"Obviously someone's calling you at home. It might be the Eileen Reynolds you were concerned about. If you're willing to pay my expenses, I'll find her and I'll investigate her. How's that?"

He took a deep breath and grimaced. He stared at nothing, thinking. "Normally that wouldn't be necessary. This has happened before. But this time it is more troubling. There is a little more to it than I've been telling you."

"What is it?"

"I've been getting weird newspaper articles in the mail. Some crazy stories about murders that happened fifty to a hundred years ago."

"Murders having to do with Saxony Skirts?"

His face changed. He scrutinized her. The look was frightening somehow. "How the hell would you know that?"

The waiter came by with a ready smile. Without even a glance at the man, Robby waved him away furiously.

"In a minute!"

"It's common knowledge around the company," Sandy said evenly, "that some women died in the factory fire years ago because of carelessness and the horrible working conditions of women in those days."

"No one proved that Saxony was to blame. You women never let go of your little ready causes, do you?"

Unruffled, Sandy continued. "You are aware then that there's a huge scandal surrounding the Eliza the Slasher murder of William Saxony. But the rumors were that the Eliza myth was embellished in the press at the urging of the Saxony clan. They wanted to make her out to be a monster."

"She was a crazy woman."

"No, she was an aspiring typewriter who was showing great promise. Too much promise. She was a threat to the company."

"Why?"

"Because she was a woman. And women, especially at Saxony Skirts, had no place for promotions. But let me tell you, Robby, you should be very concerned about the P. Rutherford who has been calling you."

"Why the hell should I?" He stood up and turned away. "This conversation is over."

Sandy didn't move. "Someone named Penelope Rutherford was highly suspect at the time of William's murder. This someone was protected from the law because of who her family was. In private, though, certain persons tried to rid her of her demons. It was some kind of exorcism, or something close to it."

He winced.

"Because she was the real murderer of William Saxony," Sandy continued.

"Who cares about all that anyway?"

"Obviously someone wants you to know about her. The same someone who killed Elizabeth Marx. And the only way we will find Elizabeth's murderer is by exploring this convoluted past of Saxony."

Robby stood up, knocking over his chair. The only other couple in the room barely looked up. This was a highly secluded restaurant for couples who didn't want to be seen. Some were having affairs, others dalliances. Sandy needed to figure out how to get out of this situation. She glanced around, trying to calculate a way out of the place, just in case. Unfortunately, she had no idea exactly where the exits were. The view out the windows looked out onto some sort of fields. She recalled seeing a solitary farm house on the way in. That was it.

Robby paid the bill.

"I'll pull around the car," he said, storming out.

Standing by the glass front doors Sandy waited anxiously. How was she to get out of this situation? Soon the black Jaguar screeched up to the front.

Could she go through with this? Or would she lose her edge with this self-indulgent man? Her power lay in her attractiveness and in what she'd discovered about Mr. Robby Saxony. His attraction to women was either because he was intrigued by them, for a while, or totally intimidated by them.

Now she had to think quickly. She had at least got her bearings. "Could we stop at Dryckars Pharmacy? It's on the next corner."

He grinned. "Sure thing. I understand."

Sandy had known Mr. Dryckars, the owner of the pharmacy, since she was a little girl. If she remembered correctly, there was a back door that opened out into the alley. Moving swiftly through the hygiene section and perfume aisle, she found the back door. In the middle of assisting a customer, Mr. Dryckars nodded and smiled as she hurried past.

Robby Saxony sat out front, drumming his fingers on the steering wheel impatiently, his mind trying to conjure up the face of this Eileen Reynolds he was supposed to know. Was she another quicky over a weekend business trip? Maybe to one of the company sites? Ridiculous, he thought. Why do women hang on all the time?

*****

It was still dark when Sandy snuck into the office the next morning. She brought along a small flashlight. She would not turn on any office lights for a while.

Shining the flashlight around the edges of the sealed door, she traced her way up and around each angle. Then she shined it through the old skeleton key lock. Very strange, she thought, to have kept this old lock. Then she knocked on the door with her ear to it. The response was simply a heavy thud, confirming that the door was several inches thick. Very solid too, she thought.

"My God, aren't you the most hard-working little administrative assistant I've ever seen," Amanda Saxony said from behind her.

Sandy whipped around. Straightening up, her flashlight beamed directly into Amanda's eyes.

"I came in early, Amanda. I was just curious to know if this was another supply room."

"Are you low on supplies, Sandy?" Amanda asked too blandly. "I'm surprised since you've been working so closely with Robby."

"What's that supposed to mean?"

Amanda grimaced. "Forget it," she said. "But after what happened to your little friend Elizabeth, I'd watch your step."

The timbre of the woman's warning struck a harsh chord. Sandy was dumbstruck, silent. She didn't move.

"Come on," Amanda said. "Let me help you out."

Sandy followed, feeling alarmed but driven by curiosity.

Amanda, wearing her usual sharp slacks and tailored jacket walked over to the wall. She reached inside a small safe and withdrew a key.

"Let me enlighten you a bit, Sandy," she said. "Follow me."

Sandy tried to temper her anxiety, counting in her head to ten, over and over. The distrust of the Saxony family went back many years. And co-workers had warned her about the Saxony deviance on her first day of employment. Oddly, the energy she absorbed from Amanda was abrasive and controlling. She had also heard from some of the executives that Amanda never took no for an answer. If someone disagreed with her policies, they were quickly transferred to another site or quietly fired from the company.

Amanda stalked over to the mysteriously locked door. Giving it a tug, she pulled as she turned, then kicked the base of the door with one square-toed boot. The door opened.

Sandy followed her in. The telephone rang on one of the administrator's desks and she whipped around. She couldn't tell whose desk. She checked her watch—5:30 A.M.

"You see?" Amanda blurted suddenly. "Here's a prime selection from the pictures dear old William used to take."

"William was a photographer?"

Amanda smiled. "He thought he was. The problem, you see, was that he developed all his own shots. In those days they used cyanide in part of the developing, and he went slowly insane from the repeated use of it. Eliza the Slasher didn't have to murder him. He would have done it to himself soon enough."

Sandy looked around quickly, nodding, wishing so much that Jan or Glenda were there with her to take it all in. She spotted a pile of photos nearby and picked one up. "It looks like he enjoyed photographing the ladies," she commented. "Some of these are clearly pornographic."

Sandy flipped through one shot after another of women wearing lacy outfits, barely covering their bodies. And she knew the face of one model shown repeatedly.

"In fact," Sandy said under her breath, "it is Penelope Rutherford in these pictures."

CHAPTER ELEVEN

Amanda turned on her. Her eyes flashed. "And what do you think you know about Penelope Rutherford?"

Sandy was taken aback. "I've heard information here and there."

Amanda scrutinized her. "From whom would you hear anything? I suppose you know about Eliza Mortimer?"

"Eliza the Slasher? Sure. She's the one who was hanged for William Saxony's murder. The newspapers heralded her as the woman killer with the 'brutality of a man.' It was highly sensationalized."

Sandy feigned naivete. She didn't know where to go with the conversation. Then Amanda started talking again.

"Eliza the Slasher, that's right. Look at all these," she said walking over to a pile of articles and clippings. "It's all in the history of the company. Eliza had guts. She didn't like management. She took action. Shows she had some kind of drive, don't you think?"

Amanda's tone had become tense. Sandy swallowed hard. Amanda waltzed about the room, indicating articles and plaques on the walls like a museum curator. "Eliza was no pushover," she stormed, "she was an infamous murderer driven to madness and mania, a woman scorned wielding a bloody axe." She paused. "The only problem was, she was not the murderer of Mr. William Saxony."

Sandy turned slowly, raising her gaze imperceptibly. Amanda hardly saw her, her drive to tell the story was so intense. The sound of her high-heeled boots scraped the wooden floor as she walked. The only light in the room was that emanating from a small green bankers lamp she had flicked on upon entering. Amanda knew her way around the room. And around her Saxony history too.

"Eliza Mortimer's only crime," she continued, her voice a resounding force now, "was that she was a lowly, entry-level type-writer, you know, a typist. But she was also someone who wanted to move up in the company. Now, not only was it unheard of for a

107

woman to want to work outside the home in those days, but it was doubly strange that she wanted to move up. Well, she and William were soon romantically involved. This was not her choice of course. But Eliza was a climber. She had plans."

"Sounds like she might have had a motive too. For killing William Saxony."

Amanda whipped around and grabbed Sandy's wrist in a firm grasp. "There was someone much more dangerous that William Saxony hadn't counted on."

With that she threw herself back into her voluminous leather chair on wheels and it shot back across the parquet floor. She was continually adjusting her watch, checking the time, and turning it around and around on her wrist.

There was a lull now in the excitement. After a pause, Sandy said, "But I thought Eliza was hanged for the crime?"

"She was, she was," Amanda chirped, spinning around in her chair. "But the press dubbed her 'The Slasher.' Believe me, the ones that coined the name were the same damn people who knew the truth! The truth would complicate a lot of lives, believe me—not to mention the status of the Saxony family."

Sandy paced a small path by the door, trying not to appear too curious. Then she realized several photos had fallen to the floor. Leaning over, she picked up a photograph of Penelope Rutherford, but in this shot her hair had turned stark white. Her eyes were tormented and wild. One eye appeared markedly larger and more round than the other, and a small cyclone seemed to rush through her expression.

Amanda said nothing. She merely smiled, a disquieting knowing smile as she got up from her chair and moved next to Sandy, gazing at the photo over her shoulder.

"Now, those are the eyes of a murderer."

"What happened to her? She's a young woman in this picture, but look at her hair? It's all frizzed out and white."

"Of course it is. She endured something horrific."

Sandy was quiet. Amanda grinned. Her mouth had a twisted delight about it, as if savoring this story brought it back to life.

"Do you know of Dodie Carmichael?" Amanda asked, raising her voice as if angry.

Sandy looked around. She couldn't lie. Not to this woman. "I've heard a bit."

"From whom?" Amanda turned on her, grabbing Sandy by the arm. "From Robby?"

"You're hurting me."

"He has no interest in the truth about the company. He'd never admit that women died working for the damn name or that women have been prevented, by any means necessary, from moving up."

This seemed to be a deranged outburst. Should she agree or not? Run out of the room? "I know about the fire," Sandy finally said. "Is it your belief that the Saxony company took no responsibility for the accident when the women died?"

"Take any responsibility?" Amanda laughed bitterly. "Are you kidding? In fact, old William Saxony, the president of the company at the time, blamed it on what he called the 'irresponsibility of women—women he claimed were working long hours because they couldn't get their work done during the work day. He said this was due to their inability to handle office work and that they 'should not have left their domestic jobs at home.' The truth was, he had them working around the clock to be competitive with other clothiers at the time. Too many men in charge," she said, knocking over a stack of photographs with a sweep of her hand.

Genuine fear came over Sandy for the first time since the horrible murder of Elizabeth Marx. Then a sudden banging came from behind them and she turned.

"What the hell are you two doing in here?" Robby barked, storming into the room. "You just had to know, didn't you, Sandy?"

"We're out of here, dear brother," Amanda retorted. "Sandy was just interested in a history lesson about the good old boys club called Saxony. Calm yourself."

"Why would that be?" he pressed, his tone annoyed. He left Amanda's office and, once back in his office, threw his briefcase down. "I have a ton of work. If you'll go to your desk, you'll see a pile I left for you. I need the proposal done by nine- thirty."

"It's only seven o'clock Robby," Amanda retorted. "Her work day hasn't officially started."

"Stay out of it. Sandy knows she owes me."

Sandy grimaced. Amanda gave her a stern look. Her eyes went

to Robby then back to Sandy. She stalked out of the room.

Sandy spoke to Robby in a whisper. "You still want me to get on those two phone calls? The ones about Eileen Reynolds and P. Rutherford?"

He looked preoccupied as he massaged his forehead temples with his fingertips, deep in concentration. Then he rose and sauntered over to her desk.

"Find where that woman is located. That's first. Then I have reports for you to type. And," he said, leaning over her desk once she was seated, "I don't appreciate being blown off like last night. I don't know who you think you are."

With that he walked into his office and slammed the door. Sandy grinned in spite of her nerves. Checking around, she stood up and walked quietly to examine the assistant's desk next to hers. They had yet to hire someone to replace her old position but she did recall some booklets coming in from the branch offices that could be in the desk.

Flipping through the booklets, she studied the photographs of the group pictures, searching for the name Eileen Reynolds. Still the procedure confounded her. Why would this woman be harassing Robby? It did seem strange. And to call him at home? That was a sign of imbalance and crossing the line. Whoever she was, she was definitely trying to shake him up. Did this woman know of Robby's reputation with the ladies? All the ladies he could get his hands on? But what a way to start a career at a new company.

Finally her search was rewarded. At the small branch in Taylorville, about forty miles south of Chicago, she found the name E. Reynolds listed. However, there was no picture. Was it because she was new to the company? Or did she not want to be photographed for a more insidious reason? Sandy picked up the phone.

"Yes, this is Sandy Larson from the corporate office. I'm the assistant to Robby Saxony. Is this the Human Resources Department?"

"Yes. That would be me. I'm Betty. How may I help you?"

"I know this will sound odd. I need a photograph of a new employee at your branch named Eileen Reynolds and I need any information about her that you can fax to me."

"I know she's pretty new. Is there a problem with her work? We really like her. She was recommended to us."

"Recommended? By whom?"

"Let me see," she said over the sounds of flipping papers in the background. "Someone in your office. That's all I know."

"Well, any information you can give me would help. The order is right from the top. Robby Saxony needs all the information, including the photograph. How soon can you get it to me?"

"I'll fax it through right away. What's your fax number?"

Ten minutes later Sandy waited by the fax machine located just outside of Amanda's office. This would be tricky. She hated to wait for any confidential fax outside of Amanda's office. Interestingly, Amanda had insisted that the fax machine for both her and Robby be placed there. Why not have her own fax? But Amanda preferred, for some reason, to share a fax with Robby. It seemed important. So, of course, Sandy's phone rang. It was located twenty feet away, on her desk. She let it ring. Then Amanda's door swung open.

"Aren't you going to get that? Let's not let calls go into voice mail."

"I know," Sandy said, but she didn't move.

Amanda glared at her. The fax machine grunted.

"I may as well get this fax. It's coming now."

Amanda frowned. "It will be here after you get the phone."

The phone stopped ringing. At the same time, the fax spurted from the machine. Amanda shook her head and stormed back into her office.

Soon Sandy spotted what she expected—background and resumé on Eileen Reynolds. Papers in her trembling hand, she perused them quickly. Then she reached for the last page, still looking left and right. The photo came through, more in black hues than in light. Immediately, a chill raced through her when she recognized the eyes, the aquiline nose, and the chin, and soon the entire visage of Eileen Reynolds wearing glasses. Eileen Reynolds also known as Eliza Mortimer.

For a moment, Sandy clutched the photograph, as if it were alive and needed to be tamed. Then she raced to her desk and phoned Glenda. Glenda's answering machine kicked on.

"Glenda," Sandy said to the machine, looking around her desk, "it's Sandy. I'm at work over at Saxony. Here's the latest. Robby asked me to explore the background of someone named Eileen Reynolds. But listen, it turns out this Eileen Reynolds has a face identical to Eliza Mortimer's. I swear it is her face. Call me."

Robby whipped out of his office suddenly. "I need these done in half an hour."

Sandy eyed a two-inch pile of papers he'd thrown on her desk. "Fine."

*****

Jan hadn't slept the night before. She hadn't slept the night through in a week. Now as afternoon evolved into early evening, she thought it was getting dark too soon. Fall would soon be winter and this was always the first sign.

Walking to the front hall closet, she decided to take a walk in an effort to sleep well later on. Yet as soon as she'd stepped outside and had pulled her scarf tightly around her neck, she saw her again. Tears spurted in her eyes. Frustration? Cold? Fear.

Tucked behind a tree on the Saxony property, a small but prominent figure emerged. Jan squinted, trying to see. The woman wore vintage clothing and her hair was wild and frizzy. Her long dress reached the street, dropping around a pair of pointed toe boots. Around her neck she wore a fox stole and she had on a high-collared blouse and a matching tailored jacket. On any other person, Jan may have figured she was just an eccentric or an actress on break from a play. But this person, this was a woman playing at a cruel masquerade.

Jan started to run, her Nike tennis shoes hitting gravel, the waist on her sweat pants loose from recent weight loss. All the tales of exorcisms and the trip to that bizarre cabin in River Falls became one convoluted grey vision now, this woman apparition. Several times she turned back quickly to see the small figure now running after her. Something glistened in her hand.

The air puffed out in visible spurts as Jan sped up; the sounds of her footsteps on the gravel path becoming more defined and sharp. The sound of her own breathing alarmed her, seemed to overtake her, as if she couldn't keep up with herself, or her thoughts.

Jan started to cry, not caring if the specter saw her. She stopped, her fists clenched, her eyes blurred. She'd face it, this thing. She turned. The figure was gone.

Jan turned back, her eyes scanning the ground. Then the steps again. Looking up, the wild hair bobbed in a light snowfall.

Breaking all rules of sanity, the woman now walked over to Jan. "You'll stop seeing him," she said sharply. "For your own good." "What?" Jan said, her voice unsteady. "Listen to me," the woman said. She lifted her hand in a fist, shaking it at Jan. "He's in our hands now." Jan recognized her suddenly. "Brandy? What are you talking about?"

Brandy whipped the shiny object she'd clutched in her hand at Jan's legs.

Bending over, she picked it up. It was an old-fashioned razor from what she could tell—called a cut-throat after the turn of the century. Jan gasped, all the power gone from the scream, until the fear became rage.

Once inside her coach house, she leaned back against the door, pressing her hands flat against it as if to keep evil forces out. The telephone rang. She couldn't move. The answering machine kicked on.

"Jan, it's Sandy. Meet me at the Glen Ayre diner. It's really important." Jan still didn't move, afraid to pass in front of the window where the shades were up. "Glenda called me," Sandy's voice continued. "We have to meet. Now, don't think she's nuts, but Glenda believes the spirits of Eliza Mortimer and Penelope Rutherford are alive."

CHAPTER TWELVE

That evening, Jan stumbled into the Glen Ayre diner. Glenda and Sandy were huddled toward one another, talking quickly, seated in a corner booth. Glenda waved Jan over.

Jan was out of breath. "I got your message. I was too frightened..." She didn't finish.

She stood over the two women, swaying from side to side.

"Jan, have you been drinking?" Sandy asked, knowing Jan's tendency to "self-medicate."

"So what if I have? What does it matter anyway? They're going to get me—one or the other of them!"

Even amidst silverware clatter, her voice permeated the small place. Several well-coiffed older women sniffed reprovingly in her direction. Sandy reached out and gently pulled Jan into the seat.

"What's happened?" Sandy asked.

Jan just kept shaking her head. Her hands were trembling and her mascara was smeared.

"She's still following me. But it's worse than before."

"Who?"

"Brandy Saxony is playing at something or she is something. I don't know."

Jan's voice trailed away. Sandy and Glenda exchanged a look.

"She is stalking me dressed in old clothes. Her hair! Her hair is wild and—she threw this at me."

Jan held out the razor in her trembling palm. Glenda took her by the other hand, and patted her shoulder.

"Calm down, Jan," she said. "I hear you and I think you're right. The fact that Brandy had me drive to River Falls to appraise the antiques I found pretty strange. I always try to accommodate clients. But it was odd that there was such a specific place where she wanted the antiques delivered to—it was some sort of storage space at the

115

edge of town. So clearly, she had planned to keep it a secret from Robby. She appears to be obsessed with the Saxony history and I'm sure it relates to money. I think that's her ultimate goal."

"But why is she obsessed with me?" Jan said, her voice sounding pained. Tears brimmed in her eyes.

Sandy shook her head. "God, this makes me mad. These damn Saxony people think they can do whatever they want. By the way, I had a harrowing dinner with Robby the other night."

Glenda turned to her. "Sandy? You know there's a murder investigation going on. And Robby, although out of the police suspect loop for now, is, in my mind, still the biggest suspect. It's not safe for you to be associating with <u>him</u>."

"I knew you would be mad. But listen to this. I have something to show you." She spread the fax pages out on the table. "This is the resumé and background on one Eileen Reynolds —a woman who has been harassing Robby. Imagine, someone is harassing him for once. But just look at her face!"

Glenda and Jan looked. Jan gasped.

"My God," she said, "it's that Eliza the Slasher. The one accused of murdering William Saxony, right?"

"Yes," Glenda said. "And you can add to that the photos I found of the woman who called herself Eliza Mortimer in 1923. This photo," she said, laying it on the table, "was among those I discovered in River Falls."

The photo lay there, dark and inert, but somehow alive.

"Why do you think we're still dealing with Eliza Mortimer and Penelope Rutherford?" Sandy asked.

"For some reason," Glenda began, "Brandy Saxony is trying to sustain some of the mystery about the family. First she has us go up to the cabin where William Saxony entertained his lady friends, specifically Eliza Mortimer. She had to know we would find out about Penelope Rutherford. That was her intention." Glenda turned to Sandy. "Let me ask you. How together do you think Brandy is? Did Elizabeth Marx ever tell you much about her?"

Sandy frowned. "Indeed she did. Luckily for us, her stories were entertaining—Elizabeth was very open about Brandy and Robby. She truly believed they were evil."

"Evil?"

"Yes. Evil. That was her word."

"How did you come across this Eileen Reynolds?"

"Listen to this," Sandy said, leaning forward. "Robby is being stalked or harassed, or whatever you want to call it, by someone named Eileen Reynolds. It turns out she works at one of the branch locations of Saxony. I managed to find her. She's a new employee at a branch in Atlanta. I just called the office there and they faxed me her picture and this background information."

"So someone familiar with the background of the company is trying to spook him somehow? That's a switch," Glenda said. "Now we have to figure out why."

"And not only that," Sandy continued excitedly, "someone named P. Rutherford has been leaving messages for him."

Jan had been silent for several minutes now. All at once, she grasped her hands tightly together, leaning on the table and staring at nothing. Glenda touched her arm.

"What is it, Jan?"

"It's gone too far."

"What has?" Sandy asked, sounding impatient.

"I can't take it anymore. It's all just too much. I can't help you anymore." She stood up. "I have to go," she said.

Glenda stood up too. "Jan, let me give you a lift."

"No," she said, shoving in her chair awkwardly. "No!"

Again patrons turned. One woman shook her head, figuring Jan for a drunk. Within minutes, Jan had shuffled out the door and raced to her green Honda parked on the curb.

"I'm worried about her," Glenda said finally. "I think we should stop at her house in a bit."

Sandy turned away, her nose in the air. Several young men settled at a neighboring table. One presented her with a smile but she frowned. She felt pretty for once but right now she was just too angry.

"What is it?" Glenda asked, waving to the waitress and pointing to her coffee cup.

"It's Jan. Don't be too blown away by her."

Glenda looked at her carefully. "What do you mean?"

"Let me tell you about Jan. Jan grew up in Northwoods, you know, where the corporate Saxony office is. She didn't just come to buy that coach house by accident. Jan has always wanted to live the good life in Glen Ayre. It's like she spent her existence trying to aspire to live in Glen Ayre. And then when Robby moved in and built a house across the street, she was floored."

Glenda sipped her coffee. Setting it down, she added more cream. "So, by floored, do you mean she was happy about it?"

"Understand this—everything is an event for her. It's really annoying. She exaggerates many things."

"Are you suggesting that Brandy isn't really following her? But what about Robby? Didn't you overhear him yelling at Jan on the phone?"

"Yes. But she embellishes everything. I told her about the murder at Saxony. In fact, I called her right away. And ever since, she's been acting very strangely."

"Yes, but Sandy, in her defense—she went with me to River Falls and we endured some odd occurrences, to say the least. I've known Jan for only about three years but I know she'd never have called on me if she didn't think something was very amiss. Remember, she was the one who saw Robby between ten and midnight in his garage. And at that point, she didn't even know about the murder of Elizabeth Marx. Why should you doubt her story about Brandy Saxony following her? Why would she make that up?"

"I don't know."

"And what about the razor she showed us? No. I believe Jan is genuinely frightened of Brandy Saxony."

The lights dimmed as the diner enticed late night guests. It was a little past eight in the evening now.

Glenda sat quietly, thinking. She spun her cup around between her hands on the table. "What about Elizabeth Marx? What can you tell me about her?"

Sandy shook her head, as if remembering. "Elizabeth was in law school at night. But during the day, she did anything to move ahead at Saxony, and once she started working for Robby, I think she saw it as her ticket up. But it made a lot of people unhappy at work."

"Co-workers?"

"Well, especially Amanda. And Elizabeth said that Brandy would call constantly. She was always harping about Sestina."

"Sestina?"

"Their nanny and maid. Sestina works her butt off from what I've heard. But there are also rumors that there was something very strange going on in the Saxony house."

Glenda tried to contain her interest. "Strange as in family relations? Or some odd occurrences?"

Sandy leaned forward, looking left and right for any eavesdroppers. "For a long time, there's been a lot of suspicion around Brandy and her activities. But what Robby doesn't know, which Jan told me, is that Sestina is in on the activities too."

"Now you're calling it 'activities.' What is it exactly that's going on? Is it some sort of organized ritual?" Glenda held her breath.

"Exactly. That's the word Jan used. You see, the reason she's become so spooked is because she's become obsessed with the Saxony family."

"Overdone it?" Glenda said, setting her coffee down, "as in spying on them?"

Sandy frowned and nodded. "You bet. She claimed these alarming events happened while she was out taking a walk. Said she witnessed some wild occurrences in Brandy's basement. Jan snooped around the neighborhood. She never stayed for long because it scared her to death. It's been going on for a couple of years. Jan saw Sestina in the basement at the same time. You see, Brandy used to be very cavalier about things, if you know what I mean. And she didn't fit the mold of the Glen Ayre-type woman—you know, old money and refined ways. She was rough around the edges, unpolished."

Glenda smiled, staring at the black clog on her foot as it bobbed up and down. "How so? Was she mentally off? I find that curious."

Sandy leaned back in her chair and crossed her long legs at the ankles. She wore faded jeans with a hole in one knee and a red cableknit sweater.

"Look at us," she said. "Look at what you're wearing, your hair, your choice of jewelry. You're wearing a nice straight black skirt and a sweater. Your hair is long and curly. But Brandy never had any help with her image. Obviously she was pretty enough to catch the eye of Robby Saxony, but she was very rough around the edges when he met her. She had big hair like something out of Texas, her makeup was too much, her clothes were overbearing. Well, she started some sort of women's club. I'm not sure if they're a social group or what. But strange things would always happen at night from what Jan said."

"What kind of things? Meetings?"

"Well, I know Brandy convinced Sestina to join and then," Sandy said, pausing, "ready for this? Brandy pulled Elizabeth into it!"

Glenda gasped. "You told me Elizabeth and Robby had an extensive affair. So, did Brandy know about it?"

"Don't know. Jan claims she saw all three women in the basement—it has raised windows, an English basement, they call them. So you can see into the basement if you are say, waiting at the front door. This is how she claims she first saw something bizarre going on. She rang the doorbell and no one answered. So she peeked in the windows and, surprise, there were three women carrying on at something with lighted candles."

"Sounds innocent enough," Glenda pursued, her face puzzled. "Could be anything—maybe a spiritual group or support group."

"But apparently there was some old world magic or something being attempted. Whatever it was, something scared her to death. I never did find out exactly what it was."

"I think it's time for another trip to River Falls," Glenda announced suddenly.

"Exactly!"

"Why exactly?"

"Because I think Jan has become twice as frightened since you two went up there. Something has really sent her spiraling."

Glenda finished her coffee and turned around in her seat. The diner had really filled up. At the next table there sat a group of college-aged somethings wearing jeans and wool sweaters, excitedly bantering over some world topic and drinking coffee. The young women were svelte and without the worries of children and wide hips. Their minds were concentrated on exams, boyfriends, and class lectures.

In another corner a young couple was having a small argument, just explosive enough to stir attention and excite their libidos. The woman had artificially crimson hair that bordered on fuchsia. She wore black tights, high-heeled boots, and a leather jacket. She kept shaking her head and turning away while he sat with head bowed and his palms to the ceiling, as if perpetually explaining himself. They were surely apologies for infidelity or a missed date.

"We have to go back to River Falls," Glenda repeated.

Sandy was quiet. "I'm really worried about Jan."

"I want you to know," Glenda said, "what you've described has already been brought to my attention by Dodie Carmichael. She's that elderly woman in River Falls."

Sandy sprinkled sugar in her very black coffee. "I'm sorry, I think they gave me the bottom of the pot. I'm going to ask for another cup."

"Of course," Glenda said. "But did you hear what I said?"

"Yes," she said, uncertain for the first time since Glenda had briefly known her. "Dodie Carmichael lives in the house that used to be a church, right?"

Glenda nodded. "It sounds like you're describing some sort of rituals going on at Brandy's house."

"I guess I am. To be fair," Sandy confessed, "I think Sestina may have started it. I'm not sure. It seems like all the women involved are in a different world or something. Elizabeth would have been the most educated of the lot. I know she didn't come up with the idea. So I wonder how it all got started?"

"Do you know," Glenda said, "what Elizabeth was like as far as her scruples went? Do you think she started in with Brandy just to get more information? It sounds like she would have been the type to take whatever measures necessary to move up or to just get more information about Robby."

Sandy changed her mind. "No more coffee," she said to the waitress, rising. "Come on, Glenda. Let's take a walk."

Abruptly, they paid the check and left a small tip. Once outside, Sandy took Glenda by the arm. "I haven't really been able to tell anyone this, but I've been suspicious for a long time that something is not right at Saxony. I know it for a fact. And I'm suspicious that Elizabeth had something to do with fouling things up for Robby."

"Were you working on the Thursday night or early Friday morning that Elizabeth was found?"

"I worked until about six which is average at Saxony. They work their employees too hard, quite frankly. Each assistant wears five hats and is usually juggling the work of three or so associates. Elizabeth and I were the only two who worked for just one executive each. I must say, after having worked for Amanda, so far Robby is a breeze. He has an ego, but otherwise he's easy."

"So you saw Elizabeth when you left that night?"

"Yes. In fact, I said good night to her and happy birthday. She said something like, 'It's going to be great.' I heard later that there was a little party or something at a restaurant across the street. It was Elizabeth's thirtieth birthday."

Glenda nodded. "I heard that from Detective Halloran. He's on the Rosedale force. But he often works with me on these things."

"Is that allowed?"

"Doesn't matter. We've been friends for years. I help him and he helps me. He knows that Jan is a friend of mine. In fact he was there when the Glen Ayre police looked around the Saxony house on that Friday morning of the murder. He used to be on the Glen Ayre force. That's the good thing about these small town operations. Not too much distrust."

"Except at the corporations," Sandy said. "Several times I caught Elizabeth going through my drawers. In fact once I caught her in Amanda's office looking for something. I came right out and asked her. In her own way, she confided in me. She was always careful not to let anyone know her very well. So she was superficial in her speech. She said she knew Amanda was trying to get Robby's job. I said that wouldn't be news. The two have always been competitive. But Elizabeth said it went deeper than that."

"That was the last time you saw her going through your offices?"

"Yes, that Thursday. And then the party, which was either at Rudy's across the street—it's a rib joint—or Antonio's next to it. I guess it carried on until about ten, which isn't very late. One of the executives told me."

Glenda nodded. "And then Elizabeth showed up back at the office between eleven-thirty and midnight. That's precisely when they say the murder took place. I wonder why?"

"Right. And Jan is Robby's little alibi in a way. All because of her insomnia, she saw him in his garage during that precise time of night. Of course, Robby didn't go to the birthday event. He claims he worked late and then phoned home at about ten, saying he'd be home in a while. That's what he even told me. But there's another thing. He was apparently seeing someone else. There were rumors around the office."

"My God, he was juggling a lot of women," Glenda said.

"Here's the strangest thing," Sandy said. "I received this invitation anonymously in my mail at work."

CHAPTER THIRTEEN

"An invitation?" Glenda asked, taking it from her.

"Look at this," Sandy said.

> Please join us as we remember the woman
> Who survived the fire
> Through her death we abandon all
> quests away from hearth and home.
> at The Church—River Falls

"That's tomorrow," Glenda said.

"It's got to be that strange house that used to be a church. I really want to get to the bottom of this."

"Let's think a moment though," Glenda said, watching her feet as she strolled along, the crunch of fall leaves under her feet. "The story seems to be that we have Elizabeth Marx going back to the office for some reason at eleven-thirty. She is subsequently murdered. However, we think someone—probably not the murderer—changed the clothes of the dead body of Elizabeth into clothes that were much like Penelope Rutherford's. The connection, or the message, is that Penelope Rutherford is the one we really should believe killed William Saxony. And now we discover she survived that horrible fire back in 1903."

"So she survived the fire first, and then she killed William."

"And she killed William for any number of reasons—retaliation for the fire, for one. But the connection to the present day is that someone felt it necessary to dress Elizabeth in those clothes. Someone wanted to turn our minds back to the past, specifically, to the history of the Saxony company."

Sandy nodded. She shoved her hands in her trenchcoat pockets. "But everyone back in those days thought the murderer was Eliza the Slasher."

"Because," Glenda picked up, "Penelope's family was wealthy and could afford a cover-up. But now someone wants you to come and honor this bizarre woman Penelope. And at the very house where the family had tried to exorcise Penelope's demons, in the basement of the place."

Sandy sighed. They approached a corner with a stoplight and waited for the walk sign. Usually in Glen Ayre not more than ten cars passed through, and in fact, several times the women could have crossed. But both were deep in thought. Glenda kicked leaves and studied the toe of her clog, while Sandy stared down the street.

"I know it's hard to know whom to trust right now. I should go with you," Glenda said. "An assistant and co-worker of yours has been murdered and your best friend, Jan, saw the prime suspect across the street at the precise time of the murder. Convenient but unfortunate. And we have to deal with a spoiled wife, a maniacal executive named Amanda, and Robby, the arrogant boss."

"Not to mention Sestina," Sandy added, "the scary housemaid and nanny. And then there's John Mills. He was another co-worker of Robby's who had an interest in Elizabeth, but she wouldn't have anything to do with him. He wasn't high enough at the company. And he wanted Amanda's position in a bad way."

"Where was little Charlie the night of Elizabeth's murder?"

"As far as I know from Jan," Sandy said, "he was at home in bed. Sestina stayed up late to watch after him. Sometimes she stays overnight."

Glenda shook her head. "And yet everyone in the house claims Robby was gone all night. Where was Brandy really? Did anyone talk to the other women she was supposedly out with that night? She certainly had enough motives to want Elizabeth out of the way."

"Do we know if she knew about the affair?"

"She did," Sandy answered.

Then she shook her head as they raced across the street. "But why did Brandy have Elizabeth in this private club she had going?" They reached Glenda's old car. The two women had disseminated and analyzed a good deal of information. Glenda stood there a moment, jiggling her keys in her hand. These were the only sounds breaking the silent fall night. The sound of the keys clanked clearly, all the more loudly in the cold.

"Let's leave tomorrow," Glenda said to Sandy's retreating back.

"I think Jan should come with us," Sandy said, unlocking her small Honda across the street.

Glenda nodded and got in her car. She rolled down the window. "Give her a call. But I don't think she'll be willing to go."

The next morning, Sandy pulled up in front of Glenda's Stickley-style bungalow and parked out of the way of the Volvo.

"Jan isn't with you?" Glenda asked. "I kind of figured that would be the case. Let's get started."

They motored through downtown Rosedale, traveling on Main Street. Soon Main changed to Euclid Avenue, and they were in Glen Ayre. That's when Glenda saw them.

"Look over there in the Dominicks' parking lot," she said, pointing. "Isn't that Jan?"

Sandy scooted down in her seat. "It's Robby! It's my boss, for God's sake! What is she doing with him? It looks like they're arguing."

"She did say he was harassing her, didn't she?"

"Yes. But I thought she was exaggerating. In fact it looks like she's unloading groceries."

"Should we intervene?" Glenda asked, glancing at Sandy. "No. Let's stay low. I'm just going to pull over here a second."

The morning was very cool. It reached only 50 degrees. Jan wore a purple scarf around her neck and a lightweight trench coat. At one point she dropped a smaller bag, and apples rolled on the ground. Robby didn't move to pick them up. Instead, he continued to berate her while she bent over and scrambled for the fruits. Several other early morning shoppers, a young husband with his toddler and a woman in another car, nearby turned to look. The husband strapped his son in his car seat and walked over.

"Things are getting ugly," Sandy said.

"Let them be," Glenda said. "Let's not go over there after all."

"There's going to be trouble," Sandy said. She studied Robby and Jan. "I know Robby. He's definitely got it in for Jan."

Robby continued to rant, flailing his arms as he spoke to Jan and telling the young father to mind his own business. Jan shook her head. Her face was strained and she appeared to be crying. Then she jumped in her car and slammed the door.

The young father spoke sternly to Robby. Robby simply pointed to the man's car and waved an angry hand at him.

"Let's go," Glenda said.

The drive to River Falls was just under an hour. The two women sat quietly listening to Glenda's tapes of Beethoven and Mendelssohn.

Glenda smiled, trying to lighten up Sandy's spirit.

"I like Beethoven," she said, "especially when I'm driving. The passion motivates me."

"That fight in the parking lot was strange," Sandy said. "I mean, I know Robby bosses everyone around at the office, especially the women. But why does he have it in so much for Jan? She's his alibi, for God's sake?"

Glenda nodded. They passed an extensive pastoral scene of cows and corn. "That's the whole point," she said. "I question that alibi now." She frowned. "And I especially question their relationship."

Before Sandy could answer, Glenda leaned forward to read the next sign. "Look at the map and tell me which exit we take. I can't remember."

"Grove Road," she said.

Soon they exited and passed through the sleepy downtown vintage of River Falls. On one side there was something akin to a feed store where two townsfolk talked lazily on the doorstep. Aside from that there was no one on the street.

"I remember it's Church Street. Hard to forget. It's just past the downtown area."

Sandy was quiet. The town rested upon them heavily in some odd opaque way. It was as if they were driving through a backlot set, a preconceived plot, and not an actual small Illinois town. The sky was like a thin film draped over the scene—like a blue blanket. The sun peeked through now and then, trying to see, but everything had become grey. Even the colors of the town, the bold red awning over the pharmacy and the green sign of the liquor store, were tinged with sepia tones.

The little area was hilly. Tidy bungalows and Victorian homes lined Main Street. Glenda always found the older houses along the main thoroughfare intriguing, because at one time, Main Street had no doubt been a gravel road and hardly the imposing force it now was as it lorded over yard boundaries. Because inevitably Main Street had been widened and had become busy, needing towering stoplights. The small houses felt violated, as if their windows were portholes to the private lives led inside.

"Was there a time on that bizarre invitation for you to be there?" Sandy pulled the pink card out of her purse. "That's just it. There is no time. I guess you arrive when the moon is in the seventh house or all the moons are happy or whatever."

"You're not taking this very seriously, are you?" Glenda said. "If it gets you through, that's fine. But I think we should realize we're dealing, quite possibly, with some unstable people here."

"I know," Sandy said, eyeing the invitation in her hand. "Maybe you should drop me off there."

"Are you sure? We're here," Glenda said, pulling up across the street from the blazing red house with a vacant space instead of a steeple. "It looks pretty dark."

"I'll be fine. Just so I know you're still out here."

Glenda leaned forward over the steering wheel and gazed at the house. She turned the engine off. They sat in an interminable silence. Autumn had swept through this little town and scattered leaves in abundant eddies and swirls. A large pile had swelled into a six-foot circumference in the street in front of the Carmichael house. There was a cryptic foreboding about that.

Clearly there had been a steeple on the house at one time. It had been removed and was put to final rest in the dank basement. She thought about the stories Dodie had told her. Were they scare tactics? The crazy talk of an old woman?

"Go on then," Glenda said. "I'll be here. I'm not going."

Sandy crossed the street swiftly. She wore capri pants and a denim jacket which she pulled more tightly around her as she scurried along. Glenda had cracked the windows to hear anything she could. She watched Sandy ascend the one concrete step in front of the house. It was still the original church entrance.

The door was opened by Dodie herself before Sandy knocked. Then the two women disappeared inside the house.

The sky turned mostly grey with an autumn streak of orange. Glenda sat back in her seat. In a discreet spot, she hoped she'd not be detected. That's when she saw her.

Staring out the front windshield, she saw a petite woman with brown hair and glasses hurrying toward the house with wide strides. There was no doubt in Glenda's mind. It was the same face as that of Eliza Mortimer. The woman's gait was strange; she held her arms tightly at her sides as she trekked toward the house.

Glenda was struck with a panicked need to warn Sandy somehow. Did the other women know about her? Glenda emerged from her car quietly and crouched behind the rear passenger door to get a look.

This Eliza impersonator wore a drop-waist dress with a pleated skirt. The dress had an ample sailor collar with a ribbon tied in front. Could this be the woman who was harassing Robby? It seemed unlikely that Robby could ever be harassed.

The young woman bypassed the front door and walked mechanically to a small flight of stairs at the side of the house. These would lead to the basement. Glenda raced around the car and darted to a tree.

There was a purple light emanating from the basement. People could be seen moving about in the room.

Light seeped through the dismal grey day in occasional shots of sunlight which lasted only seconds. Glenda had a clear view of some sort of meeting below. Then she heard chanting.

"Remember the fire, the women who died —

"The Saxony reign will end when the last man falls."

Sandy was backed up flat against the outside wall. From what Glenda could discern, the players included Dodie Carmichael, the Eliza Mortimer woman, Brandy Saxony, and two other women she couldn't identify.

The chanting and reciting of passages continued for another hour. Gradually, an unexpected convergence began on Sandy. The women gathered around her with their arms interlocked. Glenda could see fear in Sandy's body movements. She had started to crouch on the floor.

Soon Glenda could no longer see Sandy. The women had closed in around her. Dodie was asking questions of the group, demanding responses. Each of the women carried a candle in one hand and wildflowers in the other. Some carried herbs instead of flowers. Their clothing was distinctive. Each of the women wore a long skirt with a white high-collared blouse.

Dodie settled into a large mahogany chair the size of a throne.

Behind the seat there were around ten pictures—blown up to wall-size, all of men. Glenda recognized the stern expressions of William, Randolph and Richard Saxony and underneath them all, the overly confident Robby Saxony.

How were all these women connected to Saxony?

Within minutes, the event turned even more bizarre. Glenda watched carefully. The sun ducked behind clouds which made her view easier without the reflection off the window.

Dodie stood up from her regal chair and started to unbutton her high-collared blouse. Glenda squinted, trying to tell if she was seeing something else. But no, within minutes, Dodie Carmichael stood there—completely naked. Her thighs were curdled with age, her breasts low.

Glenda crouched down even more, somewhat embarrassed, then noticed the rest of the women had done the same. And then within minutes, the entire assembly had donned black dresses, high-collared and Victorian.

It's some sort of funeral, Glenda thought. Except now all the women surrounded Sandy, attempting to take off her clothes.

"You must renounce your desire to work. Become one of us. We mourn the women who died in the fire of 1903. Now is the time to be reborn in the likeness of those before us. We must embrace them. We have to remember their mistakes."

With that, several women who knelt near Sandy held out a black dress for Sandy to put on. But Sandy was backed up against a far wall.

"Why are you doing this?" she asked. "Was Elizabeth a willing participant in this fanatical group?"

Dodie stepped up haughtily. "I'll have you know, young woman, that this was where we brought the great Penelope Rutherford back to her sanity. Penelope Rutherford escaped the tyranny of the damn men. Elizabeth was on the path away from herself as an aspiring lawyer and business woman. Those women were locked in the building in 1903, caught in a fire of horrific proportions. There were no fire escapes, the conditions were deplorable for any young woman."

Sandy stood up, clutching her cardigan tightly to her skin, trying to protect and conceal. "It was a travesty of justice of course, that fire and the women who died. But what are you all about here?"

"You have to know your enemy," Dodie said, her wrinkled face in a grimace. "Woman herself works against herself. Womankind must return to her rightful position. Hearth and home."

Sandy was breathing quickly, her sensations alert, her fear of this female extremist group apparent. "I know some women believe in the traditional roles, but I don't think you should deny yourself the chance to succeed in business or politics or the arts."

Sandy glanced around furtively at the women. "My mother was a surgeon—quite talented, I might add. And so far no calamities have occurred. I didn't suffer neglect because of her career. I admired her diligence," Sandy said, accentuating "admired."

Dodie shook her head violently. "We have seen reality. They—men—must be defeated. And the only way is to be aggressive. You must get them before they get you. That's the way it is. That's what she taught us."

"Who is she?"

Still outside, Glenda grew more alarmed as the women closed in on Sandy. She crept around to several full shrubs near the front door. Pulling on each of the double doors at the entrance to what had been a church, she found them both locked. She had to surprise them. Then she got another idea.

She padded to the side of the red brick structure. Downstairs, the group had moved in. Several women held Sandy by the arms.

"Stop this!" Sandy said, pushing them away. "I don't want to be a part of this cult. Why would you think I would?"

Dodie straightened up as if coming out of a trance. "You work for him, of course. You work for the devil himself. Robby Saxony has to be defeated."

"Elizabeth worked for him," Sandy said firmly. Then her face changed. Her voice was strained. "Did you have anything to do with what happened to her?"

Several women standing in the background shook their heads and whispered to one another like aliens who didn't understand the language.

"That was not us. We tried our best with Elizabeth. We tried to talk sense into her. She was sleeping with that man!" Dodie said. "She needed our help."

"That was her business," Sandy said.

"No!" someone from the back screamed. Then the women

unfolded the dim light of the candles and formed a semi-circle around Sandy. "It was not her business alone. I know because I have become an important part of this group."

It was the face of Eliza Mortimer. Or, the person who had become her. In her hand she wielded a cut-throat razor.

CHAPTER FOURTEEN

Hands trembling, Glenda managed to jimmy open a side window. As she stumbled into a hallway of the house, she was stunned by a six-foot enlarged photograph of Penelope Rutherford. The uneven eyes pierced through the onlooker. She had coils of curly bangs lying flat against her forehead and her mouth curved, twisted, bordering on both a smile and a frown. It was a haunting visage. What would possess any one person, much less a group, to idolize and follow such a tormented character?

Hands gripping the walls, Glenda caught her breath before starting down the stairs. Shadows crept into hollows here and there, like strange little puffs of smoke and drifted her down the stairs one by one.

Then all at once a scuffling of feet—wild, scrambling. A row of candles was lit, flickering and daunting in a row along a far wall. Now the women in the group were chanting or humming. The words were mumbled, a dialect she couldn't decipher. Then she heard Sandy.

"Penelope Rutherford murdered William Saxony," she cried. "Why are you all worshipping her as if she were some sort of savior?"

"She had the power, whatever you'd like to call it, to defeat the enemy. She escaped the fire," Dodie said. "She lived on after ridding the world of William Saxony. Soon it will all change. History will change. But we have to obey nature. We must return to our homes and sacrifice."

Glenda leaned forward to hear. And as she did so, a woman's face appeared five inches away from hers, and she jumped back. It was Eliza Mortimer.

"Why don't you join our little party?" Eliza said, grabbing Glenda by the shoulders.

Glenda pushed her away and raced for the chair where they'd put the naked Sandy. Plowing through the group, she saw Sandy getting up. Glenda grabbed the chair and used it to herd the woman away. Within minutes, the two had shoved the basement door open, fled outside into the side yard, and into the car.

Sandy hid on the floor in the back seat of Glenda's car.

"There's a blanket in the back there, Sandy."

"My God," she said, panting. "They're crazy, I tell you. Those women are on something."

Glenda nodded, driving seventy miles an hour down the sleepy side streets of River Falls. Without telling Sandy, she headed toward the William Saxony cabin for one more look.

"You wouldn't happen to have any clothes around, would you?" Sandy asked. "Those lunatics. I had on a new pair of capri pants too."

"They're obviously a group of fanatics. And their obsession seems to revolve around Penelope Rutherford. I now see that it was no coincidence that good old Dodie took me on a personal tour of the place — where Penelope was supposedly healed of homicidal demons way back when."

"Yes, but Glenda, they believe her power was her malevolence, and I think old Dodie thinks it's carrying on to the present—that there's some sort of force radiating from the Rutherford woman."

Glenda nodded. "Sometime you should take a closer look at the photo of Penelope. Her face looked tormented. But in those days, people didn't know what to do with mental illness. They interpreted her insanity as some sort of preternatural power. That's all I can think of."

Soon she pulled up the long driveway to the Saxony cabin. "Let me check in here quickly for some clothes for you."

"Where are we?" Sandy asked, sitting up enough to look out the back window.

"I'll be right back."

Glenda jumped from her car and raced from cabin window to window, trying to find one ajar. Without any luck, she walked across the front of the porch, peering in the windows. The place had been cleared out.

She turned to leave. The afternoon light waned as clouds closed in. Then in her peripheral vision she paused; a flash of light had come from within the house. The floor creaked loudly where she stepped.

Turning back, she jiggled the front door several times. Someone was in the cabin. Just as she thought this, the door suddenly whipped open. Glenda stepped back quickly.

A diminutive blonde wearing spandex pants and a turtleneck stood as a silhouette in the frame of the door.

"Sestina?" Glenda said. "What are you doing here?"

And then, from behind the nanny, little five-year-old Charlie Saxony walked up.

"We are here on vacation. Do I know you?"

Glenda pulled herself together. "I'm sorry, no. Someone pointed you out to me. I'm a friend of Jan Gate's," she said.

Sestina frowned. "Ms. Gates is no friend of ours. She is a meddling problem for our family."

"Your family?"

"The Saxony family," she said, fighting her accent. "They are my family too."

"May I talk with you for a moment?"

Sestina hesitated. Then she leaned over to Charlie. "Go and find your Legos, sweetie. Play in the back room."

Charlie shook his head. "I don't like that room! What if the lady comes back?"

Glenda felt a chill run up her spine.

"It will just take a minute. Go. Now."

Sestina pushed the screen door open to let Glenda in. Charlie was still clinging to Sestina's leg. Sestina wandered to the kitchenette and poured out a cup of tea. "Would you like a cup?"

"Yes, thank you. But first of all, I have a friend resting in my car who is in need of some dry clothes. She took an accidental dip in the lake. Are you familiar with the beachfront about a mile down the road?"

"Why would she go in the water?" Sestina asked suspiciously.

"I'm afraid she slipped. Her name is Sandy Larson. She works for Robby."

"Yes, of course. Bring her in."

Glenda descended the creaky steps of the cabin and darted to the car. She opened the back door.

"Sorry I took so long. Sandy, I've managed to locate some dry clothes."

Wrapped in Glenda's quilt, Sandy nodded and got out of the car. Glenda found her plucky attitude somewhat astounding after what she'd been through.

"Sandy. I'm sorry about what happened to you at the party."

"You mean, the ritual of the witches of Salem? I'm fine, for God's sake. I just want some clothes. I'm sure even if I went to the police, no one would believe me."

The two women trekked up the slight hill to the cabin. Sestina held the screen door open for Sandy.

"I have only some clothes I found in a trunk in the spare room," Sestina said in her broken English. "I'm sorry."

Sandy nodded. "God knows I wouldn't fit in your clothes," she said. "I'm Sandy Larson. I don't know if you remember me, I met you once at the office."

"Of course." Sestina was exceedingly polite.

Soon the three women were seated and sipping hot tea. Glenda glanced at Sandy sympathetically. Sandy had been forced to wear a floor-length skirt and a high-collared blouse.

"I appreciate the clothes," Sandy said ironically, wiping dust off the skirt. "Quite the fashion plate, aren't I?"

Glenda turned to Sestina. Charlie was throwing colored Legos around in a far corner of the cabin.

"Sestina," Glenda said, "what do you know about Brandy Saxony and her activities while you're up here on vacation? Do you know where she is now?"

Her blonde hair pulled back tightly in a pony tail, Sestina's round face turned and she eyed Glenda carefully. A major decision was taking place in her mind. She glanced back at Charlie who played alone on the floor.

"Jan has indicated," Glenda began, "that things seem to be falling apart over at the Saxonys. I wouldn't be so bold as to ask if there hadn't been a murder. And Jan saw a lot of activity on the night of the murder. She's heard the arguments." Glenda stopped, eyeing Sestina. "You must want something better for Charlie. Do you know about Brandy's involvement in some sort of cult around here? It meets here in River Falls."

Sestina stood up, looking small and wispy, and walked to the pot on the stove to pour in more hot water. She wore high clunky shoes and her thighs and figure were as slight as a girl of twelve.

"I care about Charlie," she said in a hoarse whisper. "And the strange things I've seen up here are foreign to me. I figured it was part of the American culture I didn't understand. Mrs. Saxony seems to have her reasons for what she does. Mr. Saxony is seldom home and when he is, they fight and fight. To be honest, it is as if Brandy stays in the marriage for another purpose than that of love."

Glenda nodded, giving Sandy a glance. "What do you mean?"

Sestina swallowed hard, staring at the steam rising from her tea. A strand of thin blonde hair fell in her eyes. Both of her tiny hands clutched the teacup.

"Funny thing is," she said, "I packed us for the trip— simple things, you know, like mugs and cooking utensils. But she—but Brandy, I don't know, her mind is never on Charlie or the family. Her mind is on whatever goes on here. Here in the town of River Falls."

She glanced at Charlie who had stopped throwing Legos. The small flames from the candles on the table wavered and flickered as a sudden breeze wafted through the room. The temperature dropped suddenly, harshly.

"Drafty old cabin, isn't it?" Sandy said, rubbing her arms.

Glenda rubbed her hands together, thinking. "Sestina," she asked, "what about Amanda? How well do you know her?"

"Amanda Saxony?" Sestina stopped. "What was that?" she said.

Glenda and Sandy looked around

"Where's Charlie?" Glenda asked, standing up quickly.

She raced to the front door of the cabin and pushed open the screen. He was nowhere on the porch or anywhere nearby.

"Charlie!"

Sestina was behind her immediately. "My God. Where is he?"

Sandy looked around the kitchenette just as Glenda hurried to the door of the spare room.

"I don't remember shutting that door," Sestina said, her voice shrill.

Glenda jiggled the doorknob furiously, then pushed with her foot. "It's locked."

"It's never locked," Sestina said. "Charlie! Answer us!"

Then there came a small voice. "It's the lady."

The three women froze.

"Break the damn door down," Sandy said, stumbling forward in her long skirt.

Glenda decided on another tack. Scurrying out the front door, she raced around to the back of the cabin to the window which led to the room. Forcing the old wood, she finally jammed the window open. The boy's eyes were wide. He didn't speak. In the corner a flicker of light glowed from a small candle by the door. The room was basically empty except for a small table and some dated toys.

"This was where we examined the antiques on our trip up here," Glenda said, turning around once in the room.

Sandy lifted her skirt. "Let's get out of here."

"Sestina, will you be all right waiting here for Brandy?"

"I must stay. Charlie and I will wait here."

*****

Jan slipped out of her coach house back in Glen Ayre. As she looked up, she felt the dominant presence of the Saxony house across the street. She saw no signs of Sestina rushing in and out with Charlie on the way to buy groceries or pick up dry cleaning for Robby. Then she spotted it—a small light blazing in the left turret of the house.

Once in her car, she flipped the heat all the way up and backed out of her small driveway. As she shifted the car into drive, she pulled on her seat belt.

As she pulled away, she spotted a purplish light flashing on and off in a turret of the Saxony mansion. A signal. It struck her that it resembled something like Morse code, like something from a light-house. But she couldn't decipher it. She drove on.

Being the first to arrive at the studio, she entered a clean spacious area with single ballet bars and mirrors all about the room. Spending only ten minutes in the dressing room, she pulled on pink tights and a leotard and slipped into black ballet slippers. In the studio again, she nodded at the matron who putsied about dusting the hardwood floors and wooden bars. Jan stretched on the floor. Rising, she placed her foot on the lower bar, and extended her leg slowly, leaning over with one arm reaching over her head. All at once, as she straightened up her small frame and pulled her blonde hair back in place with a hair clip, she saw his reflection in the mirror.

Motionless, she stood there, frozen. The man was tall and thin, too thin, and his clothes were tailored. He wore a straight-cut lengthy jacket with a starched white shirt and a very proper white tie. On his head he wore a bowler hat and had a generous but thin mustache.

His eyes upon her were determined and fierce, yet calm somehow. Jan was completely still. Her eyes searched in the mirror for the cleaning matron but didn't see her.

Turning a half circle, she stretched forward extending her arms up over her head in a long stretch. Still with her leg on the bar, she straightened up again and casually checked the mirror. Her heart beat so hard she could feel her chest pulsate.

The man was gone. Jan relaxed, letting her arms wilt at her sides. Two other slim dancers had entered the classroom. The matron was visible again and was cleaning up in the powder room. Jan walked determinedly to the wide window which let out onto a lush green park across the street. She looked out, left and right, without seeing anyone.

The class normally freed her mind from her obsessions— obsessions about Robby Saxony and Brandy. Brandy Saxony and how unworthy she was of Robby, with her simpleton background and drunken nights out with the girls. And she had a son. A child. A son and a large home and Robby and, still, she seemed to hate the life.

Hadn't she spotted Sestina and Charlie piling into the Lexus truck just the day before? Was Brandy sending her son on a vacation by himself? If Jan had ever had a chance for such a life, she wouldn't have thrown it away.

Jan went up on her toes in a releve, mimicking the instructor. She felt a roll of tension recede from her neck as she stretched left and right, eyeing the instructor even though her mind centered on Sandy and her job. Sandy worked directly for Robby. Surely she had noticed how strangely he'd been acting?

Jan drilled herself about the night of the murder. Did she really see Robby in the garage? The first time was around eleven going on twelve. And then again early in the morning. But how could she be sure about him?

Surely, Robby didn't remember that night in the August humidity, the heat, the night in the park when he'd been the first to kiss Jan

139

twenty years before. They'd been out on the tennis courts in Rosedale. Robby was just another boy in the neighborhood back then. Of course everyone knew the Saxony family, the family that lived in the largest house on ten acres in Rosedale. Old family money and company ownership allowed for horse stables, swimming pool, and trampoline for the kids.

Exhaling, Jan faced the mirror while the rest of the class took a water break. Wiping her brow with a towel, she remembered that Amanda and Robby were the gruesome twosome. Everyone knew who they were. If you had to compete against Amanda in gymnastics, as Jan had once had to do, it was common knowledge that Amanda would have all the best coaches and all the best equipment.

Likewise in later years, Jan thought, leaning forward now and looking at the tiny crow's feet around her eyes in the mirror, the competition in the game of boyfriends was also bitter. Amanda had her hair highlighted at Paul Glick on Michigan Avenue, wore nothing less expensive than designer blouses and leather pants, and drove her own Mustang convertible. Jan had always contented herself with a new pair of Levis a year.

The class resumed. With her feet turned out in first position, Jan watched the instructor. Her anger was rising within her. Soon her entire face and neck were flushed red. She couldn't get the Saxonys out of her mind. Why had this family always controlled her life? And why was it that Robby and Amanda had always troubled her in particular?

Amanda and Robby were the same in many ways—ruthless in business and life, perfectionists who only settled for the best.

Jan adjusted her ponytail, still thinking. What bothered her now were their differences. Although Robby knew he was a Saxony and wore it well, Amanda seemed to act more like one. She carried the Saxony presence from head to toe.

The class ended. Jan sat cross-legged in front of the mirror and warmed down. She closed her eyes and breathed slowly. Deep cleansing breaths.

"It was the company fire of 1903 that made everyone in town hate them," said a woman from behind her.

Jan whipped around. The matron stood there, dusting the wooden ballet bar with a cloth.

"Hate whom?"

"The Saxony family," the matron continued with an ironic grin. "I been thinking about the Saxony family a bit lately. Don't know why."

Jan's pulse raced. Could she trust this woman?

"Did you see a man, Margery?" Jan asked. "Outside the window? There was a strange man standing there."

"What man? Now you need to calm down, ma'am. You know, now with that murder over at the Saxony company place. Everyone is jittery."

Jan took in the woman quickly, visually, studying the lined dark face and black hair pulled back. She wore a baggy floral dress with an apron over it.

"So I suppose people have decided it was a murder, haven't they?" Jan said.

"Yes, ma'am. You bet. That's what that family has always been about."

"What do you mean?"

Murder.

"The fire, of course. You know, when all those women died at the hands of the Saxony company. I've lived here and my family has lived here all the way back to the days of the early Saxonys. Murder is in their blood."

CHAPTER FIFTEEN

"I've heard about the fire. It was on a smaller scale compared to the Triangle shirtwaist factory fire in New York, wasn't it?"

Margery nodded, turning away to wipe the bar behind her. "Smaller town, I guess that's all. Same amount of heartache though. Not only that, but more, as my grandmother Bessie passed the story on down to us. We were the working class that no one around town seemed to care much about. In fact, Grandma Bessie told the story how the fire may have been purposely set. Just so old William could get rid of a few problems."

Jan's mouth was agape. "Really?"

"Yes. Let me tell you—Eliza the Slasher—they say that's what really got her ire up. The fact that old William tried to get rid of his problem by having some thugs set a fire."

"You mean he had the fire set purposely to do away with some women? But why? What did they do to deserve that? That's horrible. In fact, I thought there was a special late shift of workers trying to make extra money on the night of the fire."

Margery began dusting quickly when two dancers wearing street clothes and carrying their tote bags over their shoulders breezed past her to the exit.

"Yes," she continued in a whisper. "And guess who he had working the very same shift?"

"Eliza Mortimer?"

"The Slasher. Can't blame her for cutting him to bits."

Jan shook her head and yanked her sweatshirt around her shoulders. Now she was afraid to look up to the windows just in case he'd appear again.

"The boxes," Margery continued. "Let me tell you. Box after box."

"Boxes?"

"Caskets, my dear. Numbered caskets with all the women who had died from inadequate ventilation and not enough exits. Horrible working conditions would be cause enough to hate the Saxony family. But then to have rumors persist that the fire was purposely set..."

"Do you know if there was a Penelope Rutherford in the fire?"

Margery's face froze. Her expression was grim. "I don't think I can talk about that any more," she said. "I shouldn't have started it."

She shuffled off to a closet. Searching for a dust pan, soon she was sweeping the floor vigorously, as if to wipe away the conversation.

Jan stood behind Margery, her fists clenched.

"She was in the fire, wasn't she?" Jan said, standing behind Margery. She still had her tote bag slung over her shoulder, the sleeves of her sweatshirt around her neck.

Long silence. Only the sounds of sweeping and the sight of the matron's apron as she bent over and swept debris into a dust pan. Slowly, she straightened up and turned.

"She shouldn't have lived. Not with the amount of time they say she was in there. She was a witch. There is no other explanation."

Jan swallowed hard. Surely these were just the ramblings of a gossiping old woman?

"But the most frightening thing," Margery continued, her pale eyes washed out but crystalline blue, "was that they say she emerged with a full head of white hair! Her hair had turned completely white! No explanation."

Jan was quiet a moment.

"But otherwise, she survived the fire without injury?"

"That's just it, my dear. She was the last one out. But she wasn't rescued. She walked out herself."

Jan shuddered. "And is it also true," she said, "that Penelope was from an affluent family?"

Margery replaced the broom and dustpan to the closet and slammed the door.

"Of course. How else could they have been able to cover it up?"

"Cover up her dealings in witchcraft, you mean?"

"Much more than that, my dear. Rumor had it that Penelope Rutherford was pregnant. And in those days, a young woman who was pregnant may as well have been dead. She was forever scorned."

Jan nodded. Young dancers pranced into the room, stretching and

144

staring. Another class was starting. Now late morning, Jan decided to go for coffee at the Glen Ayre Diner at the end of the block. Her mind was full with pictures of cheap pine boxes holding the bodies of the women in the aftermath of the fire. Pine boxes. Then she thought of that tormented face, the eyes of Penelope Rutherford. And she thought of the photos Glenda had found.

She walked swiftly through downtown Glen Ayre. There was a park across the street. She knew if she cut through it, she'd reach the Glen Ayre Diner that much faster. Checking the street for cars, she darted across, her dance bag bouncing off her back.

The trees were bent and wispy, shedding their leaves for fall. The branches arched over her, intertwining and reaching for one another. She loved this park. It had been the park where she used to meet her boyfriend for tennis in high school, years before. Then she frowned, recalling their breakup. He'd gone through at least five other girls that semester, even gotten several pregnant, from what she'd heard. But that had always been her pattern. She knew how to pick the least kind men. She attracted them somehow. Abusive men were drawn to her. Hard to figure out, she thought. She'd always been so willing to help and anxious to please the men she'd known.

And lately all the men she'd come to know in her life mystified and even frightened her. A cold ruthless rain started.

She could see the light of the diner on the corner straight ahead. Not far now. She'd soon be there. Then she heard the breathing behind her, sounding like her, as if he or she were also running. She whipped around.

The mustache, the firm stance. And now he had one hand in his coat pocket and the other one was reaching out to her. It was William Saxony, she'd swear to that. The same face. The same stern expression. She dropped her tote bag.

"What do you want?" she screamed, her fists clenched.

He stood there, immobile. The only sounds were his feet moving among the leaves while he watched her. Somehow nature had gone completely quiet around her, as if this man's aura were a cloud consuming all life in its path.

With each of his steps, she felt her knees weaken more and her heart flutter. Finally, she turned and stumbled into a run. She fell to the ground. Tears spurted from her eyes, angry horrified tears.

145

Crawling along, she groped around for her bag without turning back. Then she ran the rest of the way to the end of the park. The Glen Ayre Diner waited, a beacon right there, in full sight. She stood a moment, panting, waiting for cars to pass.

Jan shook her head, cursing her own cowardice when a hand squeezed her shoulder.

"What?" she said, jumping.

"It's just me," Robby said. "Your friendly neighbor?"

"What do you want?" she demanded

"We need to make certain that you stick to your story. Remember?"

"What story?"

"The night of the murder. Don't play games with me, Jan. Stick to your original story. Got that?"

"But how do I know you really didn't murder Elizabeth? I'm certainly unsure about you. In many ways."

She caught her breath and could feel her face flowing hot and red as she blushed. The rain somehow shocked her senses.

"Stop being a little fool. Don't change your story. You saw me in the garage."

"Are you guilty? Shouldn't matter if you're innocent," Jan said, raising her chin to him. "I've already told you that it certainly doesn't mean you didn't have something to do with it."

The cars had cleared from the street. Jan started to cross. He grabbed hold of her arm.

"Where do you think you're going? I'm talking to you. You owe me."

The rain had grown relentless. Biting cold drops felt sharp against her cheek.

"Why do I owe you anything?"

Robby laughed. "Let's see, Jan. First off, I haven't told your landlord all your dirty little secrets. Like the weird shit you have going on at your little coach house. I doubt someone of her stature would be happy to know that you're into some crazy cult."

Jan was shivering now. She darted away across the street and crouched under the awning of the diner.

"You're crazy Robby," she said, as he jumped after her.

"The men coming and going from your place. The wild theme

parties. I've found remnants around the house. Sestina told me the bizarre books about women and the ceremonies you've been having."
"That's not me. Sestina is lying. I haven't been into anything like that. All I know was that after midnight and before 4 A.M., the night Elizabeth Marx was killed, I thought I saw you. But you could have hired someone to do the dirty deed for you!" She was trembling violently now, trying hard to stop her lips from quivering.
"Aren't you just the tough little lady? And what is big old Jan going to do to me? You have nothing on me."
"I've known you for a very long time. I know all about the history of the Saxony men. Now leave me alone!"
With that, she stumbled into the diner. All heads turned on her as she splattered in, dripping water on the floor, wiping away black mascara under her eyes.
The room had grown completely quiet. Sound came with the crash of silverware as it was dumped into the sink in the kitchen. The waitress, Dorothy, who'd worked there since Jan was in high school, eyed her, cracking her bubble-gum and making notes on a green waitress pad. A table full of teenagers laughed.
She walked quickly over to a corner table, her nose thrust in the air. Without looking at the menu, Jan ordered a coffee and a juice as casually as possible.
"You all right today, Jan?" Dorothy said.
"I'm fine. Just had an intense class at the Clark studio. You know, Edie Clark's ballet place on the other side of the park."
"I know the place. Never taken any dancing lessons myself. Who has the time?" she said, then eyed Jan. "Or the money?"
She stood there looking at Jan with the coffee pot in hand. Jan felt oppressed by the crowd in the place. Part of it was certainly her agoraphobia, but still, everyone did seem to be staring. Agoraphobia, the fear of leaving one's house or being in wide open spaces, or crowded restaurants. This disorder was normally kept in check with medications and therapy. But today Jan felt truly paranoid with Robby breathing down her back. Then he walked in.
His eyes searched the place, scouring and invasive until he spotted her. He just stared. Blatantly, boldly, then he shimmied into a seat directly opposite her, located on the other side of the entranceway. Every time she looked up, he was there, bar nothing.

That's when her confusion became acute. What were her feelings toward him? Had she really seen him on the night of the murder when she thought she did? Did she secretly want to protect him? Did she still carry intimate feelings for him?

This was something she'd never even told Glenda. Shame trailed after her, for being attracted to someone so ruthless. Robby Saxony patronized and condescended to women,—using them as vehicles in any way he could—the kind of man she'd always been attracted to.

Next to enter the place was John Mills. Jan recognized him as a fellow executive of Robby's from Saxony Clothiers. He glanced around briefly and then joined Robby at his table. She sank down in her seat. Words were exchanged between the men until Robby turned completely around, taking an extended look at Jan where she sat alone.

The events that ensued left Jan feeling confused and insulted. John Mills moved over in the booth across from Robby and Robby pointed a Nikon camera with an extended zoom lens at Jan. He started snapping pictures, one after another, simply of Jan. When Dorothy walked over to get their order, he hid the camera under the table. As soon as Dorothy walked away, he resumed shooting.

Jan stood up, left a tip, and stormed out of the diner. She ran all the way to her car parked at the other end of the park and, once inside, with the doors locked, she dialed Glenda's number on her cellular phone.

Soon she got Glenda's answering machine.

"Hi, Glenda," she said, trying to catch her breath. "Please call me as soon as you get this. It's beyond the point where I can stand it. Robby is harassing me in public. And he had that John Mills man with him from his office. I know I sound paranoid, but I don't feel safe any more. Anyway, I'm on my way home. Call me."

Within minutes, Jan had reached her little house. Scanning the street, she caught Sestina and Charlie getting out of the black Lexus truck. There was no sign of Brandy.

Jan unlocked her door and threw the keys on a small round table next to the door. The usual routine. Suddenly she straightened up and her mouth dropped open. A woman sat on her blue floral sofa. She didn't recognize her at first.

"Hello, Jan."

148

Jan couldn't speak. The woman wore a severe black dress and her hair was wild and white. After a moment, Jan recognized Brandy. She wore a wig.

"How dare you break into my house?" Jan said, stepping back as she spoke.

"You, my dear, have no clue who you're dealing with." Brandy stood up as she spoke. "I know what you think of me. That I'm just some little idiot who managed to snag Robby Saxony into marriage."

Jan frowned but said nothing.

"You have no idea the powers I have or what I and my group members have tapped into. We have the powers of someone beyond. That someone is named Penelope Rutherford and she's an important woman in my life and in the lives of many," she finished. Her voice had reached a gratingly sharp soprano.

"I'm sure you believe this Penelope person is helping you," Jan said. "What is she? Some motivational speaker?"

"No. She is so much a part of me—sometimes she is me. I am Penelope Rutherford."

There was an interminable silence.

"You're crazy," Jan said in a hoarse whisper.

"I knew what I was doing when I went after him. It was a careful plan. First, I found out where his restaurant was and I got hired as a waitress. I knew, if I could get this man, I'd be on my way. And I was right. I'll be damned if I'll let some little nothing from his childhood change any of that."

"You're using Robby?"

"Of course. He works the company for my benefit. Meanwhile, I run the women in our little group."

Brandy stood up, straightening her tiny five-foot-two frame and flipped back her odd white hair.

"You're trying to be Penelope Rutherford," Jan said. "I can see that. But why her? She was crazy. She's the one who really murdered William Saxony, the very man behind all your garden parties and manicures and fine cars. William Saxony built the empire."

Brandy strolled to the door. Her four carat diamond flashed across the room when she squeezed the doorknob with a tight little hand.

149

"Penelope was a martyr to our group. Some day you'll understand her crucial importance to all women, now and forever, who try to fight the battle in the working world. They need to give up and stay home."

"Penelope was crazy! And as strong women, you should be fighting for better conditions for working women, not insisting that women stay away altogether. You're telling them they're stronger if they seek out a man to support them."

Brandy nodded. "You still have your little graphics business? You need to find your own Robby and stay away from mine. If you would just come over to our side, see things our way, we could help you. All the answers lie in the old way of life; a woman needs to guard the security of her home—mending, grocery shopping, a clean house, seeing to the children—all these beliefs should be fulfilling enough."

"But add to that, a woman needs to find a good provider? That's archaic! Why would any modern women agree with you?"

"Because, ultimately, we're the ones in control. It's called being smart and passive."

Jan backed up to the small dining room table she had pushed to the side of the room. She leaned back on it. "I have no interest in your crazy cult. If anything, I'll fight to disband the damn thing."

Brandy left with a smirk, slamming the door after her.

*****

The digital clock on his desk had just flipped to 6 A.M. when Robby threw his briefcase onto his desk. After half an hour of shifting papers around, he decided to get up and see if Sandy had turned the coffee maker on yet. He'd told her to make certain it was ready early every morning. And if she couldn't be in at the same time as he was, he insisted she set it up ahead of time.

Racing impatiently to the coffee break area, he flicked on the light in the break room and saw the unplugged, empty pot. Frowning, Robby yanked out the gold filter and rinsed the basin. He was in the middle of fighting with the grinder when John Mills walked in.

"Good morning, boss man," John said, not without sarcasm. He still detested Robby and his blue blood inheritance of the company.

150

His pursuit and conquest of the now deceased Elizabeth Marx had been as close to stabbing Robby in the back as he could get.

"Can you believe I have to waste my time making this damn coffee? I've told Sandy to set it up."

"Anyway," John said, disinterested in discussing assistants for now, "how about that impromptu meeting yesterday? We were lucky Amanda was here to cover your ass."

Robby slipped the coffee pot onto the burner. "What are you talking about? I had yesterday off."

"Yes. And our client from California, the Frasier Company, showed up unexpectedly. Luckily, Amanda had prepared a small proposal to present to them."

"Why didn't I know?"

"Don't know, my good man," John said, pivoting away, his voice trailing off.

Robby crossed his arms over his chest and leaned back on the coffee counter. His tanned face was creased in angry thought. He rubbed the cleft in his chin then poured some coffee, spilling several drops.

An hour later, passing by John Mills's office, he glanced furtively through the glass wall and spotted him talking busily on the phone. He turned to John's assistant to leave a message for him.

"Excuse me," he said, then froze when she looked up at him.

The face was familiar. But it was an old one, someone from his past, someone he'd seen long ago. And knowing his record with women, it could have been anyone anywhere—he knew that. He was speechless.

"Hello," she said, her blue eyes wide. "I'm new here. Mr. Mills just hired me." Rising, she extended her hand. She wore silver-rimmed round glasses and had her hair pinned up. She had the same Saxony eyes he'd always known. "I'm Eileen Reynolds."

"Do you know me?" he asked gruffly.

"Know you? I know you're Robby Saxony. That's about it." She smiled. "Is there a message for John?"

"Forget it. No."

He stalked off to his office. Sandy had just arrived and was unloading her bag and unlocking her desk.

"Where have you been?" he demanded.

"It's seven o'clock," she said. "This is when I get in every morning, Robby."

"Ready for the meeting with Crossfire Industries?" John asked, waltzing up.

Robby turned, a bit too quickly. His head ached from too many drinks the night before. Everything was blurry and he felt as if he would pass out.

CHAPTER SIXTEEN

"Sandy. In my office. Now."

She recognized this tone of voice as hostile but she refused to succumb. Sandy straightened her skirt and noticed that Eileen was eyeing her. John Mills leaned against his office door, watching. The battle of power was apparently amusing to the office crowd.

Robby slammed the door after she entered. Then, without a word, he whirled behind his desk and leafed through the mass of paperwork, shifting it from edge to edge with his large hands.

"What the hell is going on around here, Sandy? I depend on you to keep track of me. Don't make me look like a fool in front of the other executives. And what about Eileen Reynolds? What did you do to find out about her? Now the crazy bitch is here. She's working for John Mills. What do you know about that?"

Sandy sat calmly, absorbing his abuse.

"Robby, I put a typed meeting schedule on your desk every morning. I can't make sure you'll always read them."

He glowered at her. One eye twitched. "At least tell me what the hell you found out about this Eileen Reynolds. How did she end up working here?"

Sandy nodded and stood up. She walked back and forth in front of the door to his office. "I found out quite a bit. Actually, her resumé described a history out east somewhere. As for her being here, they hired her on the word of someone within the Saxony company."

"Come on. You've seen those pictures. Look at this," he said, pulling out an article about Eliza Mortimer from his desk. "Clearly she is the spitting image of this crazy woman."

Sandy took the article from him and studied the picture. "Yes," she nodded. "It looks exactly like her. Maybe they're related."

Robby faced the window, running his hands through his thick black hair. She always thought he had such nice hair; for such an unpleasant person—he still had nice hair. He turned around.

"Well, what is this meeting about today? You'd better fill me in." He opened his office door, nodded at all the executives who were gathering for the meeting. "And hurry up."

Sandy stepped over to his desk and sifted through the papers. "Right here," she said. "It's the group working with that new ad agency. We really want their business because they are the best."

Eyes narrowed, he struggled to concentrate, pacing back and forth. "Why is it Amanda has been prepared for every meeting and I've been in the dark?"

"I don't know. She's been working without an assistant too."

"I want to know who exactly recommended this Eileen Reynolds woman." Then he slammed the desk with his hand. "Forget it. I don't care. Give me what I need for the meeting."

He stormed out and stopped up short when he bumped into the group standing outside the conference room. Sandy returned to her desk, watching Robby banter easily with the group. Did anyone else see his fists clenched or his foot tapping nervously?

Inside the executive conference room, "the fish bowl," as the assistants called it, all the bases were covered. Each of the five executives heading up Saxony Clothiers took seats. There was John Mills on the right, Amanda Saxony and Robby Saxony across from one another, and Tom Smithers and Gus Richman on the left. That rounded out the group.

Sandy walked into Robby's office and started straightening up the paper mess. Suddenly Eileen Reynolds strolled in.

"Excuse me, I don't think we've met formally. I'm Eileen. As of today, I work for John Mills."

Sandy stepped around the desk. Eileen wore a short skirt with a creme-colored blouse and high-heeled creme shoes. Not exactly professional. Wasn't this woman from the cult?

She extended her manicured hand.

"Sandy Larson," Sandy said, uncertain. "Nice to meet you."

"How long have you been here?" Eileen asked.

"Too long," she said laughing. "No, I've been here around three years."

"Then you knew Elizabeth."

Sandy was taken aback. "Did you know her?" she asked,

surprised.

"In a way. Some friends of mine knew her. And I met her several times. It's just such a tragedy. I can't imagine who would have wanted to kill her. Of course it didn't help that she was involved with Robby Saxony."

Sandy frowned. "That's no reason to kill someone."

"No," Eileen replied, "but it could be a motive."

Sandy returned to the desk and began straightening papers again. Any semblance of sun had long disappeared and it had turned grey outside. Eileen strolled about the office as if she were in a museum. Soon she came to the article about the history of the place and she leaned in more closely. Sandy clicked on another light on his desk so she could see. Eileen whipped around suddenly.

"That wasn't necessary. I've seen them all before. In fact, I know the history of this place and the Saxony family very well."

Her voice was low and unnatural all of a sudden. Sandy swallowed and placed several piles to one side of the desk with post-it notes in efforts to organize Robby's work. She could sense Eileen behind her, around her. Eileen walked over, carrying the plaque with the article about Eliza the Slasher with her.

"It's rumored that Robby Saxony is related to someone from the fire—a mistress who was pregnant with William Saxony's child at the time. And then, of course, the murder.

"Yes, that's what I've heard. But according to Robby and Amanda, Eliza was hanged and Penelope Rutherford was sent away to some institution."

"I don't know. You see the truth is, I don't believe Eliza was the murderer. The press just exaggerated and came up with the idea that Eliza was this horrible monster. But it wasn't true. I know this for a fact."

Sandy nodded, picking up a file from the desk and trying to look busy.

"Well, I don't know. I think Robby and Amanda don't even agree on the history of the company."

Eileen smiled, a knowing wide smile that was more sinister than friendly. "I know you're right about that."

The two of them gazed down at the article that Eileen had brought over from the wall by the window. Sandy eyed the photo of Eliza and then casually walked to the window, turned once to peek at

Eileen's hair which was done up in the exact same bun as Eliza's. Added to that, Eileen wore the same pair of silver- framed glasses that Eliza wore. When Eileen turned to look at Sandy, she put one hand on her hip and just stared.

Sandy shook off her suspicions. "Are you from around here, Eileen?"

"Very much so. My family goes way back."

"I see."

"You see," she said. "I know from legitimate sources who really had William Saxony's baby right after the fire. I also know that whoever had the baby, he or she was adopted by the Saxony family."

"How would you know that?"

Eileen was silent. "How is your mother?"

Sandy's mouth dropped. "How do you know about my mother? Well, she's fine, by the way. The cancer is in remission. They found the tumor. She was lucky."

"I don't know about that man she's seeing. I'm not sure he's good for her. I don't think she's safe with him."

Sandy had grown annoyed. She felt for certain this woman had to be playing games with her. She clutched the back of Robby's leather chair and looked at her directly. She too had had doubts about the man her mother had been seeing.

"What brought you to this office?"

Eileen didn't answer. Her clear blue eyes shimmered behind the spectacles, looking through Sandy as if she could see into the confer- ence room down the hall and commandeer the activities of the office. She strolled around the room. A frightening omniscience emanated from her. Suddenly Eileen stepped forward with her hand extended and grabbed Sandy by the wrist. Her hand was ice cold.

"You won't say a word, will you?" she asked.

Sandy was dumbfounded for a moment. Then the office door whipped open and John Mills came in and frowned at the two.

"Eileen, when I'm in a meeting, especially with the executive committee, I need you to be available. Understand?"

"Of course," she said, in a clear confident voice, then sauntered out of the office.

Racing to her desk, Sandy picked up the phone and dialed. "Glenda. Can I meet with you and Jan? It's urgent."

As she spoke on the phone, she noticed Eileen watching her intently. The expression on Eileen's face exuded omniscience as she turned away to look at her boss John Mills. John went and spoke with Gus, a fellow executive on the committee. Eileen stabbed him in the back with her eyes.

That's when Sandy noticed it. It was the same as the one from Elizabeth's desk—the small figurine they'd seen in River Falls. Ensconced in a backdrop of flames, the forefront of the statue showed a small stick figure of a woman wearing a long skirt. Eileen had it set brazenly, right atop her desk. Suddenly, Amanda appeared. The meeting had ended.

"Come on, dear. Let me treat you to lunch on your first day in the lovely cafeteria. John, you don't mind?" she said quickly. He stood by, his mouth agape. "And you too, my dear Sandy. You'll come to lunch with us?"

Moments before, Sandy had decided she was going to sneak out for lunch and talk to Jan and Glenda. In fact, they were going to meet at In Retrospect. But around Saxony, Sandy knew Amanda's demands had to be obeyed.

"Of course," she said.

And when she looked at Eileen, the latter had the same artificial smile, a cheshire grin of sorts. Why did Eileen look like she'd already eaten the canary?

Sandy dropped her lunch into her tote bag and grabbed her purse. As the three young women walked away, Brandy Saxony scurried into the place wearing a full length fur and matching fur hat.

"It's that cold out?" Sandy asked sarcastically. She detested fur and those who wore it.

Brandy simply threw them a saucy grin. She carried a wicker lunch basket and, as Sandy turned to look back from the elevator, she saw Brandy drop her coat in Robby's office. She was only wearing a red negligee. She closed the vertical blinds but not before the entire office could see her.

Sandy was still shaking her head when she stepped into the elevator. When she looked up, Eileen was staring at her blankly, fixated.

"What is it?" Amanda asked Sandy. "Why were you shaking your head?"

"Let's just say Brandy was providing everything on the menu for Mr. Robby Saxony today."

Amanda laughed. "Yes. The 'I'll wear the red teddy and see you at noon lunch'?"

Sandy was aghast. "Did you see her?"

"No."

"How could you possibly know that?"

"You kidding? Haven't we all done that once or twice?"

Still puzzling over this question, she and the other women disembarked from the elevator and walked into the small cafeteria. Ten or so heads turned—people who knew Amanda and disliked her and those who knew Amanda and hated her. The woman wielded a menacing corporate club over anyone who got in her way. As they filed into line, finding selections of cold fruit and yogurt, Amanda walked along with her hands clasped behind her back, wearing her signature black pants suit. She wore high heels which extended her five-foot-nine height close to six feet.

Amanda was indecisive. She paced back and forth in front of the cottage cheese bowls and pieces of lemon pie. She had nothing on her tray.

"Aren't you eating?" Eileen asked.

"Not right now," Amanda said. "I have my own private regimen and eating times."

The three women were soon seated close to the door. Sandy sat so she was able to see outside. It occurred to her that she hadn't yet called Glenda and Jan to tell them she'd be late in getting to In Retrospect.

"I have to make a quick call," she said, looking around for a pay phone.

Amanda gave her a stern look. "Isn't it something that could wait?"

"No. I had a doctor's appointment I forgot to cancel," she said quickly. "I'll be right back."

Studying Amanda and Eileen furtively from her stance by the pay phone, she got through to the antique store after four rings.

"Hello?" Glenda said. "In Retrospect. Our past is our inventory. May I help you?"

"Glenda," she whispered quickly, "it's Sandy." She paused to catch her breath.

"Sandy? What's wrong?" Glenda asked as she dusted off some first editions from the rare book cabinet. Jan looked up sharply from her seat on a white wicker chair.

"I've been detained," Sandy said. "But I think it's going to help solve the Saxony puzzle."

"What do you mean?" Glenda asked, pausing as several customers strolled into the shop.

"There's a new employee here named Eileen Reynolds."

"Isn't that the woman Robby was having trouble with? I thought she was located at the Atlanta office."

"Exactly. Well, she's been transferred. Look, I have to go. The evil boss lady Amanda is going to come looking for me."

"Call us and come by after work. Can you do that?"

"Yes."

Sandy slipped into her seat again, nodding slightly to Amanda and Eileen. This had to be the most macabre lunch she'd had in a long time. Eileen didn't seem real; it was as if she were a programmed machine—not human. Sandy couldn't put her finger on it.

"How did you happen to transfer to this location?" Sandy asked.

"Why by recommendation, of course. Amanda needed me closer to the center of operations."

Amanda ruminated, chewing on a plastic straw slowly. She eyed Eileen like some proud parent.

John Mills strolled past with several other executives. He glanced at the women, his face grim. He was clearly uncomfortable.

"Ladies," he said, "what's the occasion?"

"Does it have to be one?" Amanda asked pointedly.

Suddenly Robby barreled into the room, searching for someone. Immediately, he charged over to their table.

"What the hell is going on, Amanda? The Atlanta office just called me. There's something wrong in production out there. And they'd like to ask someone named Eileen Reynolds what's going on. Are you Eileen?"

Amanda took a sip of coffee, then laid the straw down carefully.

"Pull yourself together, Robby. Whoever it is, he or she is not up to speed with office procedure. I just flew to Atlanta and met with several people. We're changing our direction somewhat, that's all.

That's why we had the ad agency here yesterday."

Robby scratched his head, biting his lip nervously.

"We have to talk Amanda, now."

Amanda smiled savagely, relishing his frustration. "Don't bully me like I'm your wife or one of your submissive little assistants. I'll talk with you when I'm damn well ready."

He screwed up his handsome face into a foul expression. It was the frustration of a boy.

Amanda could not have been more content as she picked up the straw again. She turned back to Eileen.

And Sandy noticed that Eileen, oddly, never stopped smiling. All at once, both women decided they'd finished eating and stood up simultaneously. They walked to the garbage bins and set their trays on top of them, leaving Sandy behind.

Sandy sat there somewhat stunned. When she looked up, Robby was seated at a neighboring table, pounding coffee. No lunch.

Once back at her desk, Sandy didn't see Eileen anywhere. She walked over to her desk and dumped interoffice mail on her chair. Then she spotted it. There stood the figurine of the woman in the long skirt with the fire behind her. Was this part of the strange cult they'd discovered or some sort of awards given within the company? Perhaps just to the assistants?

Looking up finally, she witnessed a strange sight. Amanda and Eileen stood together staring out the window overlooking the vast Saxony property. They didn't speak nor did they face one another. But they were close together, standing side by side with their shoulders touching.

Robby raced past her and stormed into his office, slamming the door after him. Sandy mustered up courage for a moment. She knocked on his door.

"What?"

She opened the door a crack and leaned in. "I need to see you."

"I don't know which end is up around here! Why not. Come in and give me some more problems."

"Did you know," she said, shutting the door behind her, "that it appears that Amanda was responsible for hiring Eileen Reynolds? First in Atlanta, and then I guess she got her the transfer here."

"Why is that my problem?"

"Because, Robby, it is my belief that Eileen Reynolds is up to something. I don't know what, but I know it involves you."

"You're starting to sound paranoid, Sandy," he said, flipping through file folders on his desk.

"I think you need to concentrate on work for a change," Sandy said, picking up a red negligee from under the desk.

CHAPTER SEVENTEEN

"I want the most unusual items you have," Amanda demanded, stalking around the main room of In Retrospect like an army sergeant.

"We have many unusual items, I'm sure," Glenda assured her. "There's this painted porcelain elephant," she said, running her hand across the top of the sculpture. "And of course this leather monkey—found it somewhere in South Carolina. What are the items for again, Amanda?"

"They are for a fundraiser I'm having. It's for an as yet undisclosed philanthropy. Everyone will find out soon enough. Do you have anything really high-end? I mean, I'm going to be touting a new young artist I've discovered. His name is Gianni and he's just fabulous. I'm putting a lot of money into this guy."

"Just how weird are you willing to go?" Glenda queried. "I have some more items in back. I also have some unique items right from your collection. The antiques you and Brandy had me assess are still in the back room."

"Let's have a look at those," Amanda insisted. "I haven't seen what came in as yet."

She raced over to Glenda's side, her hands on her hips. "Where is the loot?"

Glenda smiled and walked to the back area of the store. Reaching in her sweater pocket, she pulled out the handful of keys for the place. Within minutes, the two women stood in the concentrated dark silence of the back room.

Amanda walked over to the corner of the room where a thin stream of light shot through a high window, too high to peer out of, providing minimal sun exposure. This was where Glenda stored delicate photographs, oil paintings, and rare books.

In a flash, Amanda was examining the unusual camera that Glenda had identified as William Saxony's.

163

"Where are the photographs?" Amanda demanded.

"The photographs?"

"William's photographs? You know about them?"

"Of course."

Glenda walked over and retrieved a small wooden box from a lower shelf.

"These must be the ones. They're quite unique."

"Of course they are," Amanda said. "This is what the family is all about. You know that, don't you?"

"What do you mean?"

"William Saxony was a crazy old bastard. He photographed his mistresses, of which there were many, in compromising and degrading ways—even by today's standards. He ran the company, he ran his wife, he ran his mistresses. Mr. Saxony was the original classic misogynist. And even though everyone believes that Eliza the Slasher was the one who did him in, I know better."

Glenda was interested suddenly. "Do you mean Penelope Rutherford?"

Amanda's face changed. Its gaze intensified. "What do you know about Penelope Rutherford?"

"Listen," Glenda said, "you have to know something because it has to do with your family, and your business. There's some sort of cult in River Falls, Illinois. It's northwest of Chicago."

"I know it well. I know the group you're talking about. It has been brought to my attention before. I think they're some little grass roots organization out to protest women in the work force or something. Has to do with the Saxony fire and the women who died. I think they're pretty harmless," she said, casting her glance down on Glenda from her high-heeled boots. "Just a bunch of fanatic women, I'm sure."

"Fanatic but well-organized," Glenda retorted. "Let me tell you, their practices are frightening. There is a sick goal at the heart of the group. I'm not sure what it is, but they terrorized someone I know. And we still don't know why they chose her."

Amanda's eyes darted around the room. She nodded absently, as if she'd lost interest in Glenda.

"I must take a lot of these items with me. They're quite valuable, you know."

"Right," Glenda said. "Just tell me what your family will be taking and what I should sell."

"Is there a light in this room. It's too dark," Amanda said.

Glenda left the room and returned with a small hurricane lamp. "Sorry. It's an old building and it doesn't have much light." She set the small lamp down, plugged it in, and it flicked on. She eyed Amanda now. A highly organized person, Amanda carried a Franklin planner over her shoulder which she now threw down on a cherry wood table. Soon, she had checked items off a list one by one.

Next, she picked up the box of photographs, pulled up a small early American chair, and sat down. As she perused each image, her face changed. Glenda pretended to be busy dusting off boxes and wiping down the small stereoscope that went with the pictures. But she didn't miss Amanda's fluctuating expressions.

"Were there any more photographs?" Amanda demanded suddenly.

"I think what you have there is all of them. Although there is this very heavy safe we carried in from the car. I don't know if you have a combination."

"I have no idea what it is," she said, and appeared insulted. "But I will get the darn thing open. That's for sure. Someone will open it for me or I'll blast it open."

Then Amanda scrutinized Glenda. "Just how well do you think you know the Saxony family, Glenda?"

It sounded like a threat.

"I know Robby only from a couple of introductions. And I've heard a lot about Brandy. But again, I've only spoken with her a couple of times. And then there's the little bit of history I heard while I was in River Falls."

Amanda's eyes widened. She had high arched eyebrows and a pointed nose with flaring nostrils.

"So you've heard the stories about the Saxony family?"

It sounded ominous.

"Yes."

"At least, what you think are the stories of the Saxony family? Let me tell you, the things you hear about the surface cover up a lot of the reality. There were two women who came into play. There was Eliza, Eliza Mortimer who was accused and hanged for the murder of

William Saxony. Preposterous, of course. The real murderer was Penelope Rutherford."

"I think I've seen more of Penelope Rutherford than I'd like. From what I understand, she survived the fire at Saxony and emerged with her hair turned white."

"That's the story, yes. But the truth, my dear, is that not all the Saxonys are really of the Saxony clan. That's the whole point. The men in the family, William and later Randolph and Richard, they were heartless, controlling men. William, of course, was simply typical of the turn of the century. But the later Saxony men, in the twentieth century, they were just cold, domineering bastards. They made sure even through the last decade that women never made it too far in the business. From the very beginning back then, Eliza tried to move ahead of her station and it was unheard of. And look what happened to her. She was set up for a murder she didn't commit. The hazards of working in a man's world. Until women are the majority in big industry, they'll just be wasting their lives working."

"I've heard about Eliza," Glenda said. "But you seem very bitter about the family. Even though you yourself are one of the executives of the firm now."

Amanda laughed, a cold ironic laugh. "You can't be serious. You, a business owner yourself? Surely you know how it is for us women. How many times have you run up against men in the industry who you know are giving you a runaround or are trying to outsmart you with pricing and inventory? Do you really think they deal with men the same way as they do with women?"

Glenda nodded. "I've actually been dealt pretty equally with both women and men in this industry. I also find that a lot of shops are run by married couples."

"You're a simpleton, Glenda."

Glenda was taken aback. Her eyes widened.

"Let me tell you this, lady, in corporations, women are still battling their way into the executive area. Sure, there are women who run companies or help to run companies, but do you know how many men don't deserve to be where they are, have gotten their positions simply because they're men?"

"I'm sure that's true," Glenda agreed hesitantly. "But at the same time, even those women who aren't necessarily held back in the office often have to deal with abuse at home. There are inequalities everywhere you look. But I try to help women in my business and in my personal life. I certainly don't bury my head in the sand about it."

Glenda was growing increasingly annoyed. But the next comment threw her back into anxiety and discomfort with this Saxony family member.

"Sometimes you have to straighten people out," Amanda said. "with whatever method required. I like to shock people awake."

"Are you and Robby close?" Glenda asked suddenly.

Amanda's arched brows didn't move. She eyed Glenda coolly. "Why would you ask me that?" she said.

Glenda coughed to cover up her nervousness. "I know my brother and I grew much closer as we grew older. I was just curious since you have such a high profile family and are involved in so much money and business, how you two get along."

Amanda turned away, the sound of her high heels echoing in the room. She gazed up at a small window in the corner of the room as if for inspiration. "We were typical children, you know. Competitive. Sibling rivalry for our father's attention. But it was really no contest."

"What do you mean?" Glenda asked, knowing full well what Amanda would say.

"My father favored Robby. Just as all the Saxony fathers had favored their sons. But in our case it was different because Robby and I were..." She didn't finish.

"Were what?"

"Nothing. Help me load this stuff. I'd like to take most of the items with me. I have a room at work where I store Saxony property. Someone tried to break into it recently."

"Really? Well, what should we move first?"

"The box of photographs. There are more photo albums underneath," she said suddenly, opening a secret drawer under the cabinet. Several books spilled out.

Glenda felt nervous that she'd not found that drawer before now. And now important Saxony information was being taken away. She felt the answer to Elizabeth's death slipping away. It might have helped Jan, who had been sinking deeper and deeper into an odd depression.

In an instant Amanda was standing in front of In Retrospect, the trunk of her black Mercedes coupe already open. Glenda raced to the bureau and flipped through some of the albums while Amanda was still outside.

Opening a large white one quickly, baby pictures labeled "Amanda" flew past and other family photographs. There were large group photos back from the early twentieth century depicting Saxony "picnics" and "parties" and "vacations in the Hamptons." The backgrounds were opulent and often showed the same massive English Tudor mansion.

Hollow footsteps sounded just outside the back room. Glenda dropped the album on the floor and kicked it away with her foot gently.

"I've been filling these boxes for you."

"Yes," Amanda said, eyeing the bureau immediately. "I don't recall leaving that little drawer open."

The question dangled invisibly in the air. Should Glenda play her hand or not?

"I hadn't noticed it was open," Glenda lied.

"Fine," Amanda said, kneeling quickly and yanking all the albums out one by one and then throwing them into a box. At one point, she lost her balance in her high heels and nearly fell.

Standing, she lifted the box, and tripped her way out the door. Glenda thought that Amanda had been in quite a hurry to get the albums out of the way. Definitely out of Glenda's possession. This didn't leave her much time. Turning back to the table, she reached under it and slipped the album out quickly. Again, more pictures flipped past as she looked. Where were the pictures of Robby? Had they devoted an entire album just to Amanda? That must be the case, she thought. But Amanda is the younger child.

Hearing the footsteps again, she pushed the album under the table.

"What other antiques do you want?" she asked, side-stepping quickly and looking up.

Amanda stood in the doorway, her black pants suit carving a slight outline against the darkness around the doorframe. She cast a sinister silhouette somehow, blending with the gray background. She seemed to be not an individual, but rather part of a vague larger entity.

Or cult? But this group was otherwordly, beyond Glenda's realm of understanding. Amanda herself seemed like one of the women she never knew well but was afraid of in her college years, the young women who seemed to know the insidious secrets of the world—and those who used that knowledge to rule those around them.

"What is it?" Amanda asked sternly from inside the shadows.

"What do you mean?" Then, "What else do you need me to move?"

"I suppose that's it. I have to go. I might be by to pick up more." With that she spun around and left.

Why was it every time Glenda encountered Amanda she felt oppressed, as if conversation with her was merely her way to gain an upper hand?

"I hope you found everything you need," Glenda said from the back door to the store.

Amanda said nothing as she whipped her long legs into the Mercedes.

Glenda raced inside and picked up the telephone. "Mindy, it's Glenda. Happy Saturday morning to you, too. Have you had to deal with Amanda Saxony lately for any reason?"

Mindy stifled a yawn. "She's been creeping me out a bit actually. She's been going on about some fund-raiser she's having. It's going to be an art show of some sort. But there's something amiss about it."

"In what way?"

"There's something really off about Amanda. Let's put it that way. She's getting some sick thrill out of whatever it is she's planning."

Glenda walked back to the storage room then. Lifting older wares off the dusty books and aged tables, she found a set of horse-shoes and a pile of victrola records. She picked up one of the records—"Let Me Call You Sweetheart."

She moved on and smiled to herself as she held an old snowshoe in her hand. She pictured William Saxony sloshing up to the little cabin of love nestled in the vast black pine trees of River Falls, wading his way through several feet of snow. She could see Eliza Mortimer standing on the front porch with one seductive hand on her hip, her white dress falling in graceful layers and folds around her slight figure.

There was something about that cabin, something restless about it. Glenda had sensed it when she was there. And she felt certain she'd experienced a preternatural aura of some sort. There was definitely a presence there. The restless yearnings of thwarted passions? Or the murderous inclinations of a haunting Eliza or Penelope?

In her reverie, she could see William ascending the small flight of stairs to the cabin, no one around to observe their intense foray beyond Victorian mores, the two having gone wild, no different than the creatures of the forest.

So who was to say that woman on the porch was Eliza? Glenda unfolded the black and white picture in her mind; Eliza Mortimer standing with her hand on her hip and her proper spectacles. Certainly appearances could be deceiving. But what if Miss Eliza had been a stooge? Someone set up to take the fall, as the saying goes. But why? And for whom? Was there truth to the Penelope theory? A life of madness and exorcisms?

Glenda heard something and jumped. A young couple poked around in the rare books section. The man looked up, smiling. He wore a University of Wisconsin hat and his sweatshirt said "Madison."

"I'm sorry. Did we startle you?"

Glenda laughed. "No. Please enjoy yourselves in the stacks. Have a look. I was just lost in thought."

She returned to the room. It greeted her with a dark cold it had never had before. The chill in the room was invasive, as if it crawled about the place in solid form. She studied the large pile of Saxony items still remaining in the middle of the floor. Even as inanimate objects, Glenda felt the Saxony family was violating a space that had once been pure, like a metaphysical rape.

Her mind shot to her fantasy again, playing it in her mind like a home movie. William Saxony had now slipped off his snowshoes and ascended the stairs. But in this vision, the woman standing there was white-haired, her eyes bulging from her tortured face. She had an emaciated figure—very thin, shapeless, and malnourished, and yet, Glenda could see in her mind's eye the control the young woman wielded over William.

Ignoring the presence she felt, she crept over to the pile of items and reached under the table. Somewhat guiltily, she laid the white album she'd kicked out of the way onto a table.

Walking to a nearby cabinet, she unlocked a drawer and pulled out the stereoscope photo she'd saved of Penelope Rutherford. Now she knew. This indeed could have been the woman who had brought William Saxony down. Eliza had been accused. Easier to convict— a common worker without a high profile family. But could that have been to cover up the real crime and who had committed it?

Lifting a set of heavy victrola albums out of the way, she uncovered a small pine desk. It appeared to be a delicate desk, not one for the man of the house but perhaps for a woman or for a younger person.

As if on cue, the bell jingled over the front door of the store. The couple had probably left. That's when she noticed a slender middle drawer in the small desk. She tried to open it but could only free it part way. Unfortunately, it was jammed. She hated to force anything old and of lasting beauty. She considered her treasures housed in her store to be part of her family, part of the fabric and history of the lives of many.

Pondering, she stepped back a moment, her arms crossed over her chest. It felt odd how fiercely her heart pounded, as if driven by the very presence of the Saxony life in front of her.

Kneeling, she reached under the bureau and pressed up on the drawer gently, hoping it was only stuck. Sure enough, near the rear of the drawer, she could feel something wedged in the back.

Wrapping her fingers around it, she realized that it felt like a figurine.

CHAPTER EIGHTEEN

Her mind jumped immediately to an obvious conclusion. It could be another one. Couldn't it? Wrestling the object free from the drawer, jiggling the wood around a bit more, she finally pulled out the wooden figurine.

Again she was struck by the carved folds of the fabric the figurine was dressed in. It was a female figure wearing a high-collared blouse with the sleeves rolled up halfway, as if she represented a hard laborer, perhaps a factory worker from the turn of the century. In an authoritative touch, the sculptor had added a long jacket to her knees which flared out in back.

Glenda touched the smoothly carved hands and ran her fingers along the pointed fire image behind the woman's shape. Mindy strolled in.

"Hello, boss lady."

Glenda turned quickly. "Mindy? You scared me to death. I'm a bit jumpy after a friendly visit from Amanda Saxony."

Mindy swept in quickly and settled into a small wooden chair with a creak. She crossed her legs. She wore faded jeans with a hole in the knee. She'd be working on inventory this afternoon. Glenda didn't mind what she wore on those days.

"Let me crawl around in the dust for you. You shouldn't be getting yourself dirty."

Glenda laughed. "You know me. 'Casual' wear is a light-weight skirt. I'll crawl around in anything. I just discovered yet another figurine from our little mystery club. You know, the little group of fanatical women who stripped Sandy of her clothes." She shook her head.

Mindy's eyes lit up. "I forgot to tell you. Amanda called yesterday. Said she'd be coming over."

"Mindy, why didn't you tell me?" Glenda scolded, but still smiling. "I could have prepared myself for her bizarre visit."

"She didn't call just to tell me she was coming. No, she kept on about this show she was planning. Some guy named Guido or Gianni is going to be featured. I guess he's some sort of artist. And she's been working intimately with him for years, she said. I've never heard of him but Amanda couldn't say enough. She's never married, has she?"

Glenda looked up, her eyes thoughtful. "No, you're right. But she doesn't strike me as someone who could share a life with anyone. You know, she's so self-centered. And a bit crazy too."

Mindy laughed. She took the figurine from Glenda and examined it.

"You know what I mean," Glenda said. "Amanda is so focused on succeeding in business. But it seems she has some hidden agenda. At the same time though, she's determined to promote some people and ruin others. I honestly believe she would do anything to get what she wanted."

"What's this photo album?" Mindy asked.

Glenda grimaced. "Now that I do feel a bit guilty about. I was helping Amanda load up her little Mercedes, and this album, well it inadvertently fell on the floor and somehow got kicked under the bureau."

"Glenda!"

"There's something strange about it. Someone has to see it besides me. Look at this." She reached for it and pulled up a seat next to Mindy. Opening up the album on her lap, she smoothed the pages with her hands in the gentle way she always handled anything old and delicate. "First of all, there are a bunch of your typical wealthy pastimes—parties, holidays, and the Hamptons. You know the type. But why is it that Robby is the older sibling but there are no pictures of him in here?"

"That's simple," Mindy said, pulling her hair back into a ponytail as she talked. "There must be another album with his history in there."

"No. And this one is really strange too. It covers the history of the family as a group. Now, my family, sometimes they would devote an entire album to one event or something, but the only books that were devoted to one person would be the baby books."

"I guess you're right. Maybe it's not true in every family. If Robby is the older sibling, that does sound strange."

Glenda paced to the other side of the room and stood looking out the window, her arms crossed over her chest. "What drives someone like Amanda? I admit she has determination, but she's ruthless. Part of me feels Amanda isn't who she thinks she is. Or, I don't know. That she's someone else."

Mindy's eyes creased, puzzled. "Do you mean she isn't a Saxony? That's not possible."

"No. She plays the part of the ultra-feminist achiever, but underneath, I feel there's a creature lurking."

Mindy eyed her employer carefully. "Why would you say that?"

"Call it intuition. I feel around her the same way I feel around some of these smaller items we have here for sale." She picked up a small ceramic box. "There's a sense of false worth— like cheap replicas."

*****

Across the street from the Saxony Skirts original factory site, another smaller factory had been renovated in record time. Ms. Amanda Saxony had taken over ownership of the property in July. Now it was November 25th. She had had the factory completely renovated, perfected, all glass, chisel, and polish just for today, the date of the show.

Jan was puzzled when she received an invitation to the exhibit. It seemed only a chosen few women had been invited. Added to that was a select shorter list of men who had also been invited.

Amanda could be seen through the vast glass exterior of the building's facade. She'd had the front doorknob and entryway completely recrafted in art nouveau style. The centerpiece of the front door was a woman's delicate face, platinum in substance, with a headdress which extended down both sides of the front doorway.

On this stellar night, Amanda wore a small black shift with a satiny collar. Contrasting with the simple elegance of the dress, she had on generous orange hoop earrings, sixties flower child-style. It was as if, Glenda thought upon seeing her, she was poking fun at the pedestrian matching of earrings with a dress.

The only men permitted to attend were Robby Saxony, John Mills, and three of Amanda's ex-boyfriends. The first boyfriend was a biker who'd parked his Harley right out front. The hog haunches of the bike contrasted with the pristine glass of the renovated factory. The biker wore a leather vest with a sleeveless t-shirt. The boisterous and colorful bears of the Grateful Dead danced across his back. His

175

left earlobe was pierced with a silver hoop earring and he wore a red bandanna wrapped around his head which made him look like some wounded soldier.

Glenda was entertained enough by the boyfriends that she had almost forgotten she'd come to see a photography exhibit.

"Do we know yet what this fund-raiser is raising funds for?" she asked Sandy.

"I'm afraid not. And with Amanda, it could be anything from the unkind treatment of hormones to the national endowment for women who drive SUVs. Who knows?"

Glenda sipped her ginger ale. She'd given up drinking for good years before. Still, sometimes at functions like this, her eyes would wander to a glass of chablis here or a cold beer there. Then she'd immediately look beyond the "glamour" and recall the dehabilitating depression of a drunk, the loss of control, and her maudlin down-swings. The end of an elegant evening in sparkling tights and sequins would turn to hosiery runs and a torn dress that cost her an entire paycheck.

So on this night, she estimated that the number of men totaled five. Glenda nudged Sandy. Jan stood next to her, demure in a beige sweater set and khakis. She was drinking chablis. Sandy wore a short red dress and sipped a heady glass of burgundy.

"What do you think, Sandy?" Glenda asked, twirling her long curls around her finger. "Is that another ex-boyfriend?"

Sandy followed Glenda's gaze to an adventurer of sorts. The gentleman was on the young side of forty-five, had shoulder- length hair, a beard, and wore a turtleneck and Doc Martens shoes.

"Definitely the starving artist type. What do you think?" Glenda repeated with a smile.

Oddly, despite his cavalier exterior, Glenda thought the man exuded some trepidation at being at the party in his own grungy way. What's on his mind, she thought. He carried about with him an air of arrogance that he was above all this.

"That must be boyfriend number two," Sandy commented. "Of course we don't know what order they came in."

"What are you two talking about?" Jan said, tapping her glass with a small pearl ring she always wore. "I don't know why I'm here. I don't even know Amanda that well."

"She knows you're a friend of mine," Sandy said. "If there's a connection to me, she wants you. For what? I don't know. The woman keeps me alert at all times lately. I feel like she's always trying to catch me at something."

"Now we just have to spot number three," Glenda said, looking left and right.

"My God. That's the only other possibility," she said, referring to a shortish man with glasses in the corner. He was stout and his height didn't exceed five foot eight.

"He definitely likes his scotch. I have yet to see that man without a drink," Sandy said.

"How do you know he's drinking alcohol?" Glenda said.

"Because I was next to him at the bar several times."

"Interesting."

"Stop it, you two," Jan blurted out, sounding on the verge of tears. "I've never trusted her and I still don't. I think the reason we're here has to do with evil, somehow."

"And there's our friend Rocko," Sandy said.

"How could we forget our security friend?" Glenda said.

"Why do you think?" Jan asked, her voice low. "Does she need a security guard for every public appearance she makes? Does she think she's that important?"

Glenda was thoughtful. "Obviously Brandy and Amanda are working together somehow."

The three women stood in a corner now, encapsulated in their own world, separate from the savvy new world of art and photography and certainly apart from the bizarre women's group that had practically abducted Sandy.

Sandy had not been the same person since the event.

"I recognize some of those crazy women," she said, looking around. "The ones from my unique little ceremony."

"The photographs, my God," Jan said walking over to them after having taken a quick spin around the floor. "They're scary as hell."

"Who is the photographer? Do we know?" Sandy asked.

"William Saxony," Glenda said firmly.

"How did you know?" Jan asked, her voice hushed.

"I had an idea there was a connection between Amanda's extremist views and her feelings about her family. William Saxony was notorious for those photographs. I think they have been a driving force in Amanda's life."

Glenda strolled around the black tile floor. The walls were all painted white, white paint on brick. The first few photographs were blown up six feet high. The first photograph was of Eliza Mortimer, wearing the same white dress and layers of lace. She wore her signature round-rimmed glasses. She had her hand placed on her hip, a lacy cuff cascading off her elbow.

The next set of pictures were of groups of women, wearing proper work wear of the day. The pictures looked to be company photographs of factory women. In one picture Eliza stood resolutely in the back row, standing next to Penelope Rutherford. Strangely, all the women in the photo stared straight at the camera, as if the photographer had some sort of hold over them. Yet out of the entire group, only one was smiling, a small sassy grin. And she looked away from the camera.

"That's Penelope Rutherford," Glenda said.

"Yes, that's her," came a strong voice from behind the women. "She was the only one who stood up to William. You know he went insane, slowly. It was the chemicals he used in his photography. It was necessary in those days."

It was Amanda. Sandy looked at her blandly. Jan stepped back a few feet.

"It's true," Amanda went on. "The longer he photographed, the more crazy he became. I think it shows in his work here, don't you?"

As Amanda walked on, she pointed out the progression of the family pictures.

"This is the family history here, isn't it?" Glenda commented, walking along. "I see these are early family photos. And here are some of you, Amanda, and your parents."

The group stopped in front of a lavish photograph of vacationers on a wrap-around porch. Most of the women were seated in white wicker furniture.

Gradually then, the photographs began to flesh out in many ways. It started as group photographs of the women workers. Then it went to single photographs of each woman who worked at the factory, one by one, in professional shots. Then the photos degenerated somewhat. Jan gasped aloud at several.

"Publicity, you know," Amanda quipped. "To show they were

cosmopolitan enough to hire women. What a joke. More like murdering them in the dark."

"My God, why is she showing these?" Jan asked.

The first one to surprise the group was Penelope Rutherford. She wore only her black full length dress, except it was unbuttoned and rolled down to her hips, leaving her breasts exposed. And again, there brewed the madness in her eyes. She targeted the camera with her eyes. Clearly, she was enticing her photographer. Although the picture was in black and white, Penelope's hair was blondish. Across her forehead was a row of curls and the remainder of her hair was parted in the middle. She had it pulled back with a large creme-colored bow.

Some of the photographs were so jarring that Sandy's nervousness made her laugh. Jan kept backing away, looking around her as if everyone were staring at her, as if they knew she was burning on the inside.

Glenda studied the photographs objectively, motives and the personality of the photograph in her mind. She jotted down comments about each, noting that the nudity crossed the line into blatant exploitation of the women.

"These women were all photographed by William Saxony?" Glenda asked Amanda who had just finished making her rounds of the room.

She turned quickly, the orange hoops flying as she did so. Her hair was pulled back in the usual overly tight blonde bun. She wore no bangs and her brows were dark and arched.

"Yes. The monster photographed them all."

While Amanda was explaining this dramatically, her toned arms outstretched, the first forty-ish man approached, the one dressed primarily in leather and a bandanna. He stood by patiently, as if calculating, somewhat away from the group. He didn't acknowledge he knew her until she stepped forward.

"Hello, dear Zachary," she said, leaning forward and kissing him lustily on the mouth. "Come here, you doll," she whispered. Then Glenda heard her say, "I know you're here because you value the group." Then louder so all could hear, "I hope you like Gianni's art as well as the very telling photography of our dear William Saxony."

He nodded, his eyes somehow severe and vacant. Then he leaned over and whispered in her ear. He wore a gold hoop in his left earlobe and a large silver crucifix around his neck.

Then Glenda spotted it.

On Zachary's enormous left forearm, precisely where a watch would hit, he had the tattoo of a woman in flames wearing the long skirt. Glenda nudged Sandy quickly, who in turn, also spotted the tattoo.

"My God," she whispered, "there are men in that crazy group?"

"Come on," Glenda said. "Jan looks a little lost."

Sidling up to their friend, Glenda touched Jan's arm. She held another glass of chablis with a trembling hand.

"Jan? What is it?" Glenda said.

Then Glenda followed her gaze up to a large photograph. It depicted Eliza Mortimer and Penelope Rutherford lounging on a divan, wearing only their undergarments. Eliza's head was resting upon Penelope's shoulder.

Sandy stepped onward to another set of photographs. They were anonymous donations depicting farm life in rural Northwoods and Rosedale when both towns were known collectively as North Woods and included several suburbs in the county.

The first photograph showed a young woman aged seventeen, seated coyishly in a plush armchair leaning on an ivory headed cane. The look on her face exuded quiet desperation and her mouth did not quite close over her slight overbite. A restrictive high lace collar adorned the dress and she wore a pleated skirt to her feet. The ensemble was entirely black.

Glenda scooted in beside her.

"My God, farm life in rural Illinois was depressing, wasn't it?" she said.

Sandy nodded. She gazed at a photograph of children.

"I like this one," Glenda said. "The children are smiling. It's freeing to see a Victorian photograph where the children are actually smiling. I think it's only because the mothers are standing in the background talking. They didn't use full rein over the young ones at that point."

"That's true. You can see that. Look at the women wringing their hands and clutching their dresses. What was their lot in life? It must have been miserable."

"Even the laundry was an all day task," Glenda said. "And the detergents were so toxic. Added to that, life on the farm was very lonely. And the infant mortality rate was high because of tuberculosis. And the poor men on the farms—there were frequent farm accidents. Countless young people lost limbs or were killed."

Glenda spun around to find Amanda.

Now the second brutish young man approached her. Amanda massaged his back, up and down, tracing his backbone with long, pink, manicured nails. This was the bearded man who looked like a professor. He wore a loose beige cardigan. Yet even as he spoke, Amanda looked past and around him. Glenda followed Amanda's gaze.

It led directly to Robby, who was talking to Jan. He was menacing, leaning over her and pressing his face into hers. Then a quick glance back to Amanda who still watched, very intently. The exchange between the imposing Robby and the increasingly submissive Jan grew to a frantic pitch. Glenda decided she would intervene.

"Jan, dear," she said, stepping in and grabbing hold of her friend. "I have to show you an exhibit on the other side of the factory. Over here." She looked at Robby who was clearly irate. "The other side of the room," she repeated, taking her by the arm.

"What was that all about?" Glenda said to her. "It looked like he was trying to force you into something."

"He insists that I know something about some bizarre club. He's very suspicious. He just kept going on and on. He frightens me. I mean, I've known him a long time but still, in recent years, he's become more and more strange. You think he does drugs or something?"

"Possibly. I think he's just an aggressive bully. Why did he think you knew something?"

"I don't know. He has been drinking a lot more lately. I always knew he was a drinker. He was Mr. Fraternity row in college. He was an Alpha Tau Omega at Northwestern."

"Not that you've followed his life or anything," Glenda said with a smile.

The two women turned back to see him studying them, his light blue eyes brutal and resolute.

CHAPTER NINETEEN

"I need to find Amanda," Glenda said.

Sandy nodded and guided Jan to the ladies room.

"I agree she needs a break," Sandy said. "I'll find you later."

Winding through gold lame dresses and opera-length pearls, Glenda spotted Amanda. This time she lingered with the third man —all glasses of wine and sexual laughter, poking her finger into his robust chest.

Then she changed her mind. She searched the great hollow glass and concrete expanse that was the room, for any of the strange women from the church and the bizarre ritual with Sandy. A stout older woman wearing a black dress and a small hat, with a feather plume sticking out from the rim, spotted Glenda's gaze. She looked away casually. For the first time since the strange events at the cabin, Glenda felt fear.

Approaching the woman, pausing several times, Glenda stepped up.

"Excuse me," she said.

The woman looked through her, her eyes steady.

"I was at the ritual at the church in River Falls," Glenda said. "As you may know, a young woman, a former member of your group, was recently murdered. I know you know who I mean. Elizabeth Marx was her name."

Her weathered face creased in thought, the woman fingered a medallion she wore around her neck.

"I have no idea, I'm certain," she said distinctly.

"You're lying to me. Why?"

The woman frowned, sucking in her cheeks.

"I'm not in any group," she said.

"How about if I tell you that whoever murdered Elizabeth has every intention of murdering again. Obviously Elizabeth disagreed with your group beliefs. Look where it got her."

"Why would you suspect someone in our group? We believe in

183

women—women who know that home and family are the center of existence."

"A women's radical group is quite capable of working on its own. They don't need to be supported by men. Your group renders them helpless. I don't believe in limiting women in any way."

Behind them another woman towered suddenly, sleek and sensuous. She stood behind the shorter woman.

"Don't you see," the woman with the feather said, "we are protecting women. The working world is not the right surroundings for women. Remember the fire! Our group is simply keeping a single front."

"You have an anonymous benefactor who is involved in Elizabeth Marx's murder."

"That's not true. Why would you speak such lies?"

"Because among Elizabeth's possessions in her desk drawer at work, there was discovered this letter that the murderer addressed to her. It reads:

> Your determination to succeed in your own way
> jeopardizes your standing in the circle of fire.
> I will have no choice but to rescind my financial
> funding of your townhouse and car. Please know too
> that your life is in danger. If you persist with your
> law school plans, and your climb up the corporate
> ladder, I will repeat — YOUR LIFE IS IN DANGER.

"That's a forgery," the taller woman said smoothly, her voice flowing like the scarf around her neck. She wore a red and black floral dress. "Our benefactor would not threaten a member."

Glenda studied the women, her cool green eyes darting from one to the other.

"Is your benefactor a member of the group?" Glenda asked pointedly.

The plumed-hatted shorter woman looked cowed. She peered up at her companion.

"We don't know exactly," said the woman in the floral dress. "We know she is a grand lady. We know she has extensive knowledge of our organization and the plight of Eliza Mortimer. Eliza saw the mistake she made in becoming a typewriter at a man's company. Eliza's mistake was that she loved and lived for William Saxony. And what did he do? He planned her death in the fire—along with numerous other women. He despised women in the workplace."

Glenda wondered how much these women really knew. What was myth and what was reality?

"What about Penelope Rutherford?" she asked suddenly.

Both women were aghast.

"She had money," said the one in the plume. "She was the actual killer of William. Women from our group tried to help her, to exorcise her evil drives."

"You both know the history of the Saxonys and you run it like a museum," Glenda said.

"Of course we do," the woman in the plumed hat said firmly.

"It's our duty to know," the other woman said. "We began as the Northwoods Historical Society after all."

"We have to keep it going."

Glenda tried to concentrate on the moment, but in her mind, other spirits danced around the conversation. Glenda felt trapped by the unified front of these women, a group that possessed some clandestine power.

"The group you're in encourages the idea that women should lack focus and drive and just float through life in some delusional bubble."

"You're wrong about us...what is your name?"

"Glenda Morgan."

"You don't know what power there is in just remaining passive— allowing the husband or man in your life to make the decisions. It frees a woman to mind her home. It really does." Glenda searched the room. Now she sensed many antagonistic eyes upon her and she felt oddly isolated. It was as if they knew—they knew she was trying to penetrate their safe shell of ignorance.

"May I help you?" a tall, handsome woman asked. She was wearing a tuxedo and white bow tie.

"I'm just trying to find out the truth about this group. It has included a murder in its operation."

The tall handsome woman's face became transformed.

"It's none of your concern. Elizabeth was warned. You don't understand us so we will not invite you to join, even though it would be in your best interest."

Glenda felt her face growing hot. She wiped perspiration from her forehead. The photograph of Eliza and Penelope loomed behind the three women now. Had it gotten bigger? The edges of the image seemed to blur.

Suddenly Amanda was ascending a small podium located in the midst of Gianni's paintings. The backdrop was a wall-sized abstract of a woman bending over backward in all blues and purple, with a thin rope tied around her neck.

"Thank you all for coming," she said, waving her manicured hands in the air, several gold rings twinkling in the setting sunlight seen through the glass windows. "Some of you know the importance of today's campaign to raise money. This is for the Women of the Fire—so we will never forget the importance of relationships—in business and between the sexes. Tonight," she said, spanning her hand up to the paintings behind her, "we share ideas between men and women. We agree, we discuss art and film, but most importantly, we co-exist in the only way possible. Please join the women of the fire for our banquet to be held in the grand hall adjacent to this room."

Glenda fell into the group of museum guests as Amanda finished her speech. Women milled about, ruminating on her ideas with cheesy hors d'oeuvres and glasses of champagne.

As Glenda turned to find Jan and Sandy, she saw the two women being led out of the room through a small doorway. Oddly, Sandy had to duck so Glenda realized the door was not full height, that it didn't exceed five foot eight. The tall handsome woman in the tuxedo had to duck also as they stepped through the door frame. The frame and the door were painted bright red.

A sudden alarm seized Glenda. Everything, everyone, was spinning with conversation, giddy laughter, talk of artwork. Some studied the photographs and others gazed upon the bizarre abstracts by Amanda's protege, Gianni.

Glenda tried to absorb herself in paintings entitled "Woman and Child" and "Mother's Secret," portraying the lives of women and more. The first painting showed two black silhouettes depicting a larger figure and a smaller one. The next was of a woman colored in various shades of blue, her head bowed as she leaned back against a cheap kitchen table with a bottle of scotch.

The tragedy was in the smaller figure, a child standing next to a table, her eyes opened wide with grief. And in the next painting, the woman's emaciated hand, with veins popping, reached for the bottle, the long fingers wrapped around the neck in a sinewy grasp.

All at once the wall moved. It was a vast sliding wall, a partition where an overblown photograph of Eliza and Penelope was hanging. It moved to the left like some gargantuan creature.

Still there was no sign of Sandy or Jan. Glenda panicked all at once. The man with the tattoos suddenly sidled up next to her.

"What's happened to my friends?" Glenda asked him, facing him squarely. She hated the tremor in her voice and the sight of the giant vision of Eliza and Penelope moving in the backdrop.

"They're with Amanda. It's cool. They're just getting a little pep talk. That's all. It's the best thing that could happen to your friends."

"You're insane," Glenda said, biting her lip at the unsettling over-sized abstract paintings hanging on the wall behind him.

The mammoth partition wall continued to move, and soon, a banquet table which measured twenty or so feet in length was set before them.

"We must remember," a woman's voice boomed over the loud-speaker, "that women are gifts to the world. And that we must protect them like fine porcelain. I've been in the trenches of corporate America and, believe me, it's a war for women."

The commanding voice behind the podium was Amanda's. And now the lights had dimmed. Behind her was a vast painting of Penelope Rutherford, her hair wild and white, her blue eyes intense, insane.

"We must also remember," she went on, "how Miss Rutherford suffered for us at the hands of a company—my family's company, Saxony Clothiers. And now it is clear that Saxony is in the hands of a woman."

Glenda gazed about the room in disbelief, her mouth agape. All the women wearing their plum, pink, and periwinkle blue floral dresses were nodding and moving forward, being sucked into the podium by some preternatural force. Glenda sensed something explosive was about to occur.

Yanking out a chair, she jumped up, a little shakily in her clogs and black jumper.

"Excuse me," she said, waving her arms and vying for the room's attention. "Listen to me. Amanda Saxony is leading you all down a path of," she hesitated, "being nothing! Women are not born to passivity. It does not have to be their lot, your lot!"

Amanda nodded at the biker man who picked up on his cue to race over and quiet Glenda.

"You're not setting the right mood, lady," he said, reaching out for her with rough hands. "Amanda doesn't like you talking so much. It's really bad for club morale."

Amanda's eyes were wild. She had put on a full-length apron over her black dress.

Glenda jumped off the chair and ducked under the table. Crouched down, she hobbled her way over to the podium and Amanda. Suddenly, Brandy was there. As soon as Glenda stood up, Brandy grabbed Glenda roughly by the shoulders and flung her to the floor. Glenda rolled away from her and jumped to the podium.

"Listen to me, ladies. If Amanda Saxony is your patron, your leader, why do you think Elizabeth Marx died? Why is that, Amanda? Why did you, leader of the Women of the Fire, murder a young woman who was doing so well at the company?"

Amanda was aghast. "That was Robby," she said, jumping up. "Robby Saxony is a troubled little man with little ideas. He has carried on the tradition of men as rulers, presidents of companies. No matter what their position, he had the final power. Well it's stopping now."

Rocko shuffled over to stand behind Brandy, and hooked one huge arm in Glenda's. He escorted her across the room and out through a door at the back.

Rocko led Glenda to a small room that had concrete walls. The room was unfinished and clearly part of the original factory. The floors consisted of wide, planked hardwood which were extensively marred and scratched. The walls were concrete, with layers of faded paints poking through.

Glenda felt along the cold walls and her heart raced wildly. She raised her eyes slowly to Rocko. She gripped the armrests of the chair he'd plopped her in.

"Why, Rocko?" she said. "Why are you involved with Brandy and Amanda in this ridiculous organization? She doesn't believe in you. If anything she's using men."

Rocko shook his head. "She's great to me."

"Who is?"

"Who do you think? Amanda. She knows what's best for everyone."

Glenda bit her lip furiously.

"If that's the case, why did she kill Elizabeth?"

Rocko shook his brutish head again.

"That's not true. If she did have her killed," he hesitated, "she had a good reason."

Shocked momentarily, Glenda stared at the man, at this massive creature whose desperate brain had grabbed on to some illusion of power in numbers and that women everywhere would simply succumb to men.

"If you believe in Amanda's theories, why the hell are you allowing a woman to be in control?"

He was dumbfounded.

"Amanda is controlling everyone from her angry and vengeful corner. Don't you see that? She detests men and women. But most of all, she detests herself."

The bizarre statement stayed there hovering in the air a moment. Glenda had to sit with it, absorb it in the small circumference of this back room of a factory. Her mind immediately went to the cult meeting in the basement of the church, the supposed exorcism and the inexplicable presence at the cabin.

"Then how do you define exactly what Amanda is?"

"She has told us," Rocko said mechanically. "She is the last in a line of Saxonys. You realize, we have to rid the family of Robby. He is what she calls our blackest nemesis."

"What are you talking about? He's her brother and he's the top executive at the company. What has she done to sway so many people?"

She was feeling at a loss suddenly. What had Amanda done to these people? Only in cryptic newspaper reports had she ever heard about such cults—the dreary descriptions of desperate souls sucked into various radical groups. The Waco, Texas tragedy or satanic rituals. These she had heard about. But to convince men that she was omniscient, and women, that they should bow down and submit to men, what a confused lot. She seemed to be conning both sides.

"We are taking Robby Saxony down. Amanda has planned it all out."

Glenda turned to address him again. His eyes were determined and fierce.

"I'm not going to do anything. I just want to tell you—murdering Elizabeth Marx was not an answer. How was she a threat, anyway?"

Five melodic tones sounded on Rocko's cell phone. It was a command. Someone was calling him.

"Come on. Now," he said.

They walked in darkness out the small door which led to the banquet room in back. She spotted Jan and Sandy at a front table. Before she could act, Rocko put a blindfold on Glenda and shuffled her out a door leading to the outside.

CHAPTER TWENTY

The road was bumpy. Gravel crushed by the car's weight was loud and every now and then a larger rock or two would shoot up and make a tinny sound off the side of the car.

Already a near-sighted person, being blindfolded made Glenda that much quieter. And Rocko had tied the blindfold too tightly. She was afraid she'd lose a contact. Regardless, she would no more attempt to talk than try and make a break for it. For Glenda, taking her vision was like becoming a Sampson in the Bible, after Delilah had cut off his hair taking away all his strength. They say the other senses can sharpen, but Glenda felt less of a person, less herself. She used her vision in every way to help her analyze the world around her. Her friends called her the "great observer."

The vehicle swerved and she was thrown violently across the wide seats. She spread her hands out to break her fall. The way she moved and the distance she slid convinced her she was in some sort of limousine.

An endless hour passed. Glenda's eyes felt moist, the skin hot from the patch. Several times she tried to peek out the sides. It recalled for her a time in childhood, when she was hospitalized at age twelve with damage to the eye from her brother's hockey stick. There had been an obnoxious and spoiled child in the next bed who complained incessantly.

Now, Glenda needed to see, more than just the identity of a whining child in the next bed, but to save her life. She had to get her bearings as to their location. But she couldn't discern which way they'd left the factory in the first place.

"May I ask where we're going?" she said, breaking the dead quiet.

Rocko grunted. "You don't need to know. Amanda wants you with her. Until the ascension is complete."

"'The ascension'?"

Now Rocko surpassed creepy.

"As soon as Robby Saxony is out of the picture."

Glenda swallowed, hard.

"And just how is she going to do that?"

Rocko laughed. It was a sickening, shallow laugh of someone who didn't really care how Amanda Saxony achieved her goals. "You do realize she murdered Elizabeth Marx?"

"I know that," he said bluntly. "But how the hell do you know that?"

"The first clue was the "women of the fire" statuette that was found on the scene. Then there was the motive. Robby would have no reason to kill her even though Amanda tried to set it up to look like he had a motive and opportunity. But someone planted the statuette there to connect it to the club."

Rocko grunted and shifted in his seat.

"So what else?"

"Amanda didn't count on our good Jan to have seen him in the middle of the night, for two hours in his garage. That ruined Amanda's plan of plugging Robby for the job." Glenda touched her blindfold and Rocko slapped her hand. "It was just itching," she said. "Anyway, Amanda, I figured out, was the one who called Robby to tell him to come to the office—then she held off, in the most horrific kind of way, in killing Elizabeth until she saw Robby's car in the lot. Little did she know that Jan had followed him there and saw him find an already dead person. That's why Brandy and other members of your ridiculous cult were following her. To tell her to keep quiet about Robby's innocence.

"Brandy of course changed Elizabeth's clothes and left the stat-uette to further the cause, but without Amanda's knowledge. Amanda was irate that it implicated the group. But then, no one really knew about the group."

"Don't bug me with all this," Rocko said. "Whatever Amanda Saxony has done, it's for the good of the group."

There it was again: the familiar epithet. Amanda Saxony could do no wrong.

"I'm telling you the truth about your beloved leader."

"Mrs. Brandy Saxony is my immediate boss."

The sounds of gravel grew in intensity.

"Shut up for now," Rocko ordered her.

Glenda flattened her palms on her lap, feeling the fabric of the embroidered black skirt she'd put on. Then she sat on her hands and listened.

The car slowed. She couldn't hear the driver at all. She assumed Rocko had gotten out of the car when she heard the door across from her slam. She leaned toward that side but couldn't make out precise words. Then a door near her opened. She felt cool fall air as it rushed in.

"Who's there?'" she said.

"Why the hell should you care? We're not sure what to do with you, quite frankly." Brandy leaned over in the open doorway.

Glenda knew the voice—the scent of Poison perfume.

"What is the allure of Amanda Saxony, Brandy? What has she promised you? Riches? Status? What?"

She heard a snicker. "All of those things, my dear."

"What I've learned about Amanda is pretty unsettling," Glenda said, half under her breath.

"What you've heard are lies. They were started, no doubt, by jealous co-workers and fellow executives."

"How about that Amanda had been very active with Dodie Carmichael at River Falls — learning all she could about Penelope Rutherford. Isn't it possible that Dodie filled her head with fantastic tales of Penelope's power as well as her very controversial involvement in the occult and witchcraft of sorts?"

"It doesn't matter," Brandy said. "We're bringing dear old Robby down. His days as a philandering executive are numbered. You see, we all know that Robby is a direct descendant of Penelope Rutherford. The immediate family, like Robby, tried to hush up all the talk of adoption of the bastard child in William's time. But of course, Amanda and I searched out the truth."

Glenda was suddenly yanked out of the seat and practically lifted off her feet by two mammoth and powerful hands.

"Move now, sweetheart."

Glenda started to walk, then pulled away and turned to where she thought the limo was.

"Don't you get it? Amanda wants to run the company and all the rest of you to fulfill her whims. You're a bunch of mindless robots."

"No. You don't know," Brandy said. "She treats me like a queen. I'm going to run Robby's house. It will be an honor to run everything from the flowers in the foyer to advising the cook on Friday meals."

Glenda stopped for a moment, yanking free from Rocko's grasp.

"It's all for Amanda, Brandy," she explained, her arms outstretched. "She wants control of Saxony Clothiers so she can get back at all the men, past and present, who she feels have taken her life from her. She wants to gain control. She's outraged that Robby has ruled Saxony, especially with her newly acquired knowledge that he's not even a true Saxony. This is her obsession with the lineage. She tried to set up her own brother for the murder of Elizabeth Marx."

Brandy stood by quietly, closely. Glenda could still smell her perfume. Suddenly Brandy slapped her. Then Glenda heard the young woman's retreating steps. Her heels click-clacked on a hard, concrete sounding floor.

As Rocko dragged Glenda along, she smelled the strong scent of Pine. Judging from the distance they had driven she figured their location to be somewhere north of Vernon Hills, possibly near Lake Bluff. Undoubtedly it was a secluded place buried in trees. She could hear the yawning lift of the wind and the scratching of branches on the windows.

A rough tug from Rocko broke her reverie. He tied her hands together.

"I hope you know you've surpassed harassment charges and gone into abduction," Glenda said, as roughly as she could. "And what have you done with Sandy and Jan?"

"Shut up for now," he said, lifting her up and carrying her inside.

Glenda fought the urge to joke about being carried over a threshold. Her fear level had elevated with the blindfold.

"This blindfold is really not necessary."

And as she said this, Rocko ripped it off her face. Her face felt hot and flushed and she was overwhelmed by glaring white.

She found herself standing in a room the size, depth, and width of a factory room. Far in the distance, Amanda was seated in an over-sized white chair, swathed in white fabric in sheets, and elevated around ten feet on some sort of platform. Amanda sat there, regal and ethereal, her smooth and muscular arms draped on the armrests and her heavily jeweled hands clutching the ends. She wore an all white tunic which was torn up the center and a free-standing turtleneck piece without a sweater attached. A wreath of delicate flowers crowned her head. Her blonde hair, usually yanked back severely, tumbled loosely in long curls around her breasts.

"Glenda," she said, "we don't ask much of you. Just to help me to take over Saxony. It's for the good of us all."

Glenda wriggled free from Rocko, still blinking in the stark white of the place. Obviously a large former storage locker, the concrete walls were painted white on all sides with vast windows spreading along the ceiling. The windows were opened wide to the fall air. It was a cyclone of fresh air. Birds flew around inside the room, perching here and there, then flying out the opened windows.

"Why is it fine for you to be in an industry and moving up the executive ladder, but not acceptable for the members of Women of the Fire to aspire to anything more? Why is that, Amanda?"

Amanda was visibly shaking. Glenda sensed some resistance breaking down.

"I have been forced by a long line of misogynists to get the company out of the dirt and back into the black. Robby is a fool. He knows nothing about running the company." She smoothed her hair back. "Can you believe Women of the Fire started as women from the Northwoods Historical Society! They'd talk about their husbands and dabble in history. I simply fueled the fire with poetic stories about Penelope Rutherford." Her eyes widened and she grew increasingly sarcastic in her tone. "They were housewives in search of excuses to be passive. Just what I detest. But you see, the Women of the Fire brought attention to Penelope Rutherford. Especially to the fact that Robby is not a Saxony."

"But why are you preaching a life of passivity to women while you're battling it out at Saxony?"

Amanda's mouth tightened. "These women were pawns to me— a means to an end for Robby's little empire. I'm no better than he is— I used these women too. What I am about to announce to Robby and his lawyers is that he is a descendant of Penelope Rutherford's. He is not a Saxony by blood. I am going to reveal that Elizabeth Marx knew this terribly private fact about him and that's why he killed her. See out there?" she said pointing a long arm out a window. "There's Jan Gates. Jan now knows that she cannot, in good conscience and for the sake of womankind, be his alibi. We are going to bury Robby."

"Robby knows he's not a Saxony?"

"Indeed," she thundered, "indeed he does."

Glenda frowned. "The truth is, you want everyone to give in to you. You're creating a society of weak, unmotivated women. Why?"

"Unmotivated?" Amanda said. "More like getting our just desserts. Did those women deserve to die in that Saxony fire? I think not. And it was a male-run company. I am working hard now so I can liquidate it. Look out the window, Glenda."

Rocko walked her over to one of the vast windows. It looked out over several acres of manicured lawn to a forest. There were rows and rows of flowers and sculpted hedges. Set at equal distance were large easels with oversized paintings.

"You see the work of Gianni. This place will serve as a retreat for these women from their mundane husbands and pathetic marriages."

Glenda eyed Amanda carefully.

"Not all marriages are pathetic," Glenda commented.

Amanda sat up straight in her vast chair.

"How the hell would you know?" she raged. "You, whose marriage crumbled to nothing."

Glenda's face was impassive. She took a deep breath.

"We're friends. We just weren't meant to be married."

"Weren't meant to be married, weren't meant to be married," she mocked her. "Jan has come over to our side. She's seeing things my way," Amanda said. "In fact she claims she didn't see Robby at all on the night of Elizabeth's murder. And of course, Brandy was with me when we took care of Elizabeth."

"You mean when you murdered an innocent woman."

Amanda pounded her fist on the arm rest and stood up. "Enough of this. You don't know. Elizabeth was trying to move up on her own. Our deal with her was that she seduce Robby and keep him busy. But she had her own goals outside our group. It just wouldn't do."

Suddenly two vast glass doors were thrown wide and an army of women wearing various flowing, floor-length dresses marched in. In the midst of the group, being carefully escorted, were Jan and Sandy. Jan had a look of delirium. Sandy was stone-faced.

All at once a mammoth dolly cart was wheeled into the place, piled high with the many antiques Glenda had carefully appraised in River Falls.

Amanda rose from her chair majestically and stepped over to the place where they were unloading the items.

"We offer these trappings from the days when men ruled our every whim. Set the fire," she said.

And much to Glenda's horror, several women approached the pile with elongated matches.

"Wait!" Glenda cried, wrenching free from Rocko. "Why in here? Why not outside, where the flames can burn longer and higher? And as women of the fire, it would be a true remembrance of how those women suffered in the Saxony fire of 1903."

Amanda stood with her arms crossed, the white sleeves of her tunic dress cascaded down, falling in generous folds.

"Perhaps you're right," she said, sounding magnanimous.

Now it was Sandy's turn to smile.

Within twenty minutes, the antiques were gathered outside and strewn recklessly into a pile. It pained Glenda to watch such a destruction of valued treasures. But, as if in measured time, within minutes, the Lake Forest and Glen Lake police arrived, surrounding them. Glenda smiled. "No outdoor fires are allowed in the neighborhood."

Within minutes, Amanda and the Women of the Fire members were read their rights.

"When will people learn?" a police officer said to Glenda.

Glenda smiled, massaging her wrists where Rocko had tied them. Sandy and Jan approached.

"We have quite a story to tell," Sandy said. "You'll want to record our statements. It's about the murder of Elizabeth Marx."

The detective nodded. Jan threw her arms around Glenda and cried.

Biography
Kathleen Anne Fleming

Kathleen Anne Fleming received a Bachelor of Arts in English/Communications from DePaul University in 1984 and also attended graduate school there for a time. Her influences include Georges Simenon, Dashiell Hammet, Raymond Chandler and Jean Rhys.

Between 1989 and 1995, she published approximately twenty short stories in various literary magazines such as the New Press, where it was chosen as best contribution for the winter 1992 issue, The Aldebaran and Friction. In 1993 she had an additional number of short stories published in a collection entitled One Impulsive Black Rose by the Dan River Press.

In 1999, she had published a mystery novel entitled The Jazz Age Murders by Creative Arts Books, Inc. She is also an active member of Mystery Writers of America. She lives in Illinois with her husband and two children.

photograph by Lisa Klare

Factory of Death

by
Kathleen Anne Fleming

Available at your local bookstore or use this page to order.

--1-931633-65-7 - Factory of Death - $14.75 U.S

Send to: Trident Media Inc.
        801 N. Pitt Street #123
        Alexandria, VA 22314

Toll Free # 1-877-874-6334

Please send me the item above. I am enclosing
$_____(please add #3.50 per book to cover postage and handling).

Send check, money order, or credit card:

Card #_____ Exp. date _____

Mr./Mrs./Ms._____
Address_____
City/State_____Zip_____

Please allow four to six weeks for delivery.
Prices and availability subject to change without notice.

- DVD that plays MP3's
        at the higher
            house.

* Come back in spring for min 12
Sam Betty Cindy Lorena Loli + three days
Betty Lee
- Computer: Internet leener organize
        get a DSL, better yet?

get a Cable Modem. On
    all the time as long
    as Comp is on.

    $45. per month for
        Cable Service - Save

* Get on long distance
* Get rid on neg people in your life + home
* So to doctor (derm) for nails?

Get 1 lg suit case + pack less
        (on wheels)
            RED

Get JP Penny Catalog.

Printed in the United States
746200002B